Her sm
This wa
small boat
woodlands t  ... nearby areas
where the pipeline was slated to run was more secure then this waterlogged excuse for a floating device.

Seated two by two, elbow to elbow, with Jake's body pressed up against hers proved to be anything but relaxing. Sitting shoulder to shoulder, thigh to thigh with him had tingling sensations coursing through her entire body.

"Did I mention this was a hunting expedition?" Jake asked close to her ear, his warm breath causing the loose tendrils of her hair to tickle her neck.

"*Hunting?* For what?"

"Alligators."

"What! Alligators!" Holly jumped up, rocking the flat boat and bumping into a couple trying to board. Jake grabbed her arm, pulling her back down next to him. The boat rocked back and forth, then steadied.

"This is a joke, right?" she hissed in his ear. She didn't want to know the answer. No way was she intentionally going out hunting for reptiles in the middle of the night.

"Nope. No joke. Come on, it's perfectly safe."

"Right!"

Before she could disentangle herself from his strong hold and step out of the boat, everyone was seated and the boat was pushed away from shore. The small motor kicked in and they were off.

Amazon Connection

by

Carol Henry

This is a work of fiction. Names, characters, places, and incidents either are the product of the author's imagination or are used fictitiously, and any resemblance to actual persons living or dead, business establishments, events, or locales, is entirely coincidental.

Amazon Connection

COPYRIGHT © 2008 by Carol A. Henry

All rights reserved. No part of this book may be used or reproduced in any manner whatsoever without written permission of the author or The Wild Rose Press except in the case of brief quotations embodied in critical articles or reviews.
Contact Information: info@thewildrosepress.com

Cover Art by *Nicola Martinez*

The Wild Rose Press
PO Box 708
Adams Basin, NY 14410-0706
Visit us at www.thewildrosepress.com

Publishing History
First Crimson Rose Edition, 2009
Print ISBN 1-60154-405-7

Published in the United States of America

Dedication

This book is dedicated to my husband, Gary, with love always. And to my family. It is also with much appreciation that I thank my writing 'buddies' Teri Walsh and Thea McGinnis for their staunch support and true friendship. And special thanks to Professor Eloy Rodriguez for his assistance with identifying specific plants found in the Amazonian Rainforest.

Prologue
Manaus, Brazil

Thomas Grapley picked up his beer and drained the cold malted liquid in one long gulp. Brazil's humidity and the torrential downpours were getting to him. He wiped his forehead on the already damp napkin. The hotel bar was noisy this evening. Too many people had come in to enjoy the American food they served. And listen to the American music. Mainly why Harold had chosen the place, he was sure. They should have gone some place quieter so they could talk. He watched his partner take another big bite of burger. The man was going to kill himself if he kept eating like that.

He cleared his throat to get Harold's attention.

"Do you think she suspects anything?" Tom asked.

"Nawh. After Daniels' speech this afternoon, she's got to be pretty pissed off at him for pulling the plug on signing those contracts. She's put as much work into this damn project as we have."

"I don't want to see her get hurt."

"If our plan works, she's gonna look guilty as hell when they find all that money *you* stashed in her account," Harold Bennett laughed. "What did you expect? Don't start worrying about her now. Once they figure it all out, she'll be exonerated. And we'll be long gone."

"She's a nice person."

"Yeah, well, you can't let that get in our way. Buck up, damn it. Like I said, if our plan works, it'll

1

be over soon."

"What do you mean 'if' our plan works? It damn well better work, Harold."

"Not to worry. It will. Just do your part."

"I don't trust Jake Daniels. Mr. Holmes must suspect something otherwise he wouldn't have sent Jake down here. I say we pull out now."

"Stop worrying, Tom. We aren't going to get caught. You heard Daniels. Holmes' wife is about to have her baby any day now and he won't leave her side. There's nothing to worry about."

"But he's going out to meet with Dr. Sanchez."

"He isn't going to get far. In fact, he's probably already sorry he came down to this insect infested swamp hole."

Thomas didn't like the sound of that. Harold Bennett might be his brother-in-law and his best friend since grade school back in Jersey, but he was beginning to feel as if Harold had gotten them in over their heads this time.

"Now what have you done?" he asked.

"You're going to love this, Tom. I took a couple of the guides aside and made a deal—raised the ante, you might say. I promise you, Daniels isn't going to get far."

Tom watched as Harold patted the side of his blue plaid polyester suit jacket. He knew the motion well and didn't like it. Harold kept a pistol hidden within easy reach at all times. He raised his empty glass toward the bartender for a refill and pushed his plate aside.

"Let's get out of Brazil, Harold. Get to Colombia like we planned. We don't have to stick around while they sign contracts."

"Don't be such a chicken-shit, Thomas. We stay in town until the contracts are signed and the money changes hands so it looks like everything is on the up and up. That way, if they do suspect anything, they'll find Ms. Newman's account first and go after her. We don't want to raise any red flags. Afterward, we can tell them all to kiss our asses as we disappear over the Colombian border."

"What if she suspects us and tells Daniels?"

"Who's gonna believe she's not involved?" Harold snickered, then took a long draw on his beer. He slammed the heavy glass down on the table. "She insisted we make all those changes to the route. Sets her up real nice. Either way there's nothing to worry about." He fingered his collar, wiping at the sweat trickling down his neck. "Make sure you transfer enough money to her account. Make her look real guilty."

"I don't know, Harold. What kind of deal did you set up with these guides?" Thomas wrung his hands, clenching and unclenching them. He could see the veins in his partner's thick neck and forehead popping out. The blue of his veins matched his jacket, his paisley skin tones had turned a deep splotchy red. Not a good sign for his brother-in-law. The man was too high strung and too over weight. "You aren't thinking about taking Daniels out, are you, Harold? We agreed no one would get hurt. Pinning the laundering scheme on Ms. Newman is one thing, killing Daniels is altogether a different matter. I don't want a murder rap on my hands."

"Not to worry. We'll be long gone and rich before they figure it out. Daniels is just going to get a little lost. I'm going to follow that bastard to make sure everything goes according to plan. Then, I'm going to pay Dr. Sanchez a visit. If I can get Sanchez out of the way it won't matter if Daniels makes it to the village or not. If the man isn't there when Daniels arrives, then Daniels won't be able to find out about the altered route."

Thomas took a gulp of beer. His hands shook. Even in the early days when they were always one

3

step ahead of the gangs back home he hadn't seen Harold this excited.

It made him nervous.

Chapter One

Just what the hell was Jake Daniels' game?
Everything had been going smoothly. So why had he refused to sign the contracts?

Instead of waiting for the elevator like everyone else filing out of the meeting, Holly took the stairs, two at a time, to her room on the fourth floor. She slammed her folder down on the glass-topped rattan table next to the sofa as soon as she swung the door shut behind her.

She'd done her homework. Harold Bennett and Thomas Grapley's reports were right on. They worked for GlennCorp. The Brazilian delegation had approved everything. So, why the hell was Jake Daniels stalling? She was on GlennCorp's side, for heaven's sake. You'd think he'd be ecstatic that Wild and Wonderful was fully in support of their project. It didn't make sense for him to come barging down only to hold things up by postponing the inevitable.

Holly brushed her bangs aside and sat down on the wicker sofa. Hot, and definitely bothered, her long, thick hair clung to her neck. She bunched it in her hand and lifted it to allow the refreshing breeze from the ceiling fan to cool her heated skin. Too bad it didn't cool her frustration as easily.

The possibility that something might not be right with the project was ludicrous.

The jarring shrill of the phone startled her. She automatically reached for it.

"Hi, Holly. Marcia, here."

Marcia Kline, the new exec Helen Mapes had

hired at Wild and Wonderful a month before Holly had left for Brazil was the last person she wanted to talk to right now.

"Helen asked me to call. Make sure things are going okay."

"Tell Helen the only problem seems to be a Mr. Jake Daniels from GlennCorp. Apparently, he isn't completely satisfied with my reports, and has refused to sign the contracts. I don't understand why. GlennCorp has only been pushing the Brazilians to use their company to build the pipeline to funnel oil and gas through the rainforest for the last two years. Suddenly they decide to hold things up."

"Did he give a reason?"

"No. Originally the route ran through several known ecological preserves and communities where indigenous natives lived, but after working with GlennCorp's two engineers, I sent them back to the drawing board and they came up with a better route."

"If it's GlennCorp's engineers, then you're right. He shouldn't have a problem," Marcia stated, siding with her.

"I've worked with the two Brazilian engineers, Mr. Biozzo and Mr. Temboni, as well. They helped confirm the alternate route. Of course it's at a higher cost, but I was assured by Mr. Bennett that cost wasn't an issue."

"What should I tell Helen?"

"Ask her to contact GlennCorp's D.C. office and clarify our position down here; see if she can find out what the hold-up is. Tell her I've given my final recommendations to the delegation, including Mr. Daniels, this afternoon. I've covered every angle and I'm confident everything is in order."

"She'll be glad to hear you're on top of things."

Holly could only hope.

Amazon Connection

"I'm not sure how soon I'll be able to contact her; I might have to wait until she contacts me," Marcia said, not skipping a beat. "Communication's sporadic. She's in some out of the way province in China."

Holly was familiar with Wild and Wonderful's China project. Thankfully she wasn't involved with it. Besides, she didn't need another assignment. She had other things on her plate. One of which was to figure out what Jake Daniels was up to.

"Do what you can, Marcia. My flight leaves on Saturday and I definitely want to be on that plane."

"That's right. Your sister's getting married in a couple weeks."

"Yes. I'll give you a call tomorrow after I've talked to this Mr. Daniels. Maybe you'll have some information from GlennCorp by then, as well."

She hoped Jake Daniels would keep his promise to Mr. Delgado, head of the Brazilian delegation, and sign contracts Friday. She wasn't going to be a happy camper if she had to delay her flight back home.

After saying goodbye to Marcia, Holly hung up, unbuttoned her blouse, kicked off her shoes, and headed for the shower. Reaching behind the curtain, she turned the nozzle on, adjusted the water temperature, then slipped out of the rest of her clothes. She stepped under the cool spray.

Ahhh, heaven.

Lathering the washcloth with the hotel's fragrant soap, Holly let the tepid water rinse the suds from her body, watching them go down the drain. Just like her past relationship with Anthony Hurst.

No loss there!

Tony was a handsome, sexy, charmer. But she'd discovered that he'd only been interested in one thing in life—to add as many notches to his bedpost

7

as possible before he turned thirty. She'd told him she wasn't interested in becoming one of his statistics, only to realize it was too late. She'd felt like a fool when she'd learned Tony hadn't missed a step as he'd gone on to his next victim. But she'd learned her lesson, and thankfully had left on assignment right after the breakup.

Jake Daniels reminded her of Tony.

She had to steer clear of Jake Daniels.

****

Sitting across from Jake Daniels, Holly forced herself to remain as cool as the tropical breeze drifting over the open café. The romantic surroundings didn't help her chaotic state of mind. She tried to make sense of how she came to be having dinner with Jake Daniels. One minute she was walking down the hotel hallway to find something to eat, rounded the corner, and ran smack-dab into him. The next thing she knew he was escorting her to the hotel's upscale restaurant.

Okay, so it was the perfect opportunity to question him and find out what the hell was going on. Now, sitting across from him, she found herself strangely attracted to him.

Think Tony. Think Tony. Think Tony.

Jake had said he wanted to talk business. Well, so did she. Their lavish, tropical Brazilian surroundings, however, didn't feel like business.

"Just how confident are you with Bennett and Grapley's findings?" He asked, bringing her back to the reason they were sharing a table.

She drew her shoulders up and sat back in the elegantly cushioned chair.

"I beg your pardon," she managed. "Weren't you listening when I addressed the delegation this afternoon?"

"I hung on your every word."

His tilted smile belied his words. Was he

mocking her?

"You doubt my conclusions, Mr. Daniels?"

"Call me Jake. After all, we are having dinner in such intimate surroundings."

She raised her eyebrows and looked into his deep teal eyes, the color of warm Caribbean pools. He had to be wearing colored contacts. No one had eyes that color for real. They suddenly became shadowed, cool. He stared back at her. A long pause ensued where the only sounds drifting around them were the subdued background music, restaurant chatter, and clanking of dishes and silverware. Holly, entranced by those eyes, could do nothing more than take in the planes of his handsome face; a face that spoke of determination.

Until she noticed the slight bump in the bridge of his nose. Obviously it had been broken. Somehow it made him seem more approachable. More sexy.

"I'm not doubting as much as I need to know your perspective on how the project is going," he broke the silence. "What problems have you encountered over the past few months?"

She blinked and felt her cheeks warm. Thankfully he hadn't been aware of the route her thoughts had taken.

She'd been there three long months already, working with his cohorts. Harold Bennett and Thomas Grapley weren't the nicest characters in the world, but hey, they hadn't overstepped the sexual harassment bounds, so she couldn't really complain.

Playing for time, trying to decide how to respond, she toyed with the appetizer in front of her. She popped a prawn into her mouth and munched it casually, letting the rich flavor pool in her mouth before swallowing.

"What is it you want to know?" Beating around the bush had never been her style. She decided to be direct with him, too.

9

She watched him pick up a prawn by its tail, dip it in the spicy cocktail sauce, then bite the end off with one smooth pull of his even, white teeth.

She'd heard people describe the visual act of eating shrimp as being sensual, but hadn't believed them. Until she watched Jake Daniels slowly, and with deliberation, suck that single scrumptious shrimp slathered in dripping sauce into his mouth. A very sexy mouth with full lips.

"Just how much actual groundwork have you done, hands-on, in the region? Have you actually walked any of the proposed pipeline trails to know they exist?"

Had he just said 'hands-on'?

Her tongue stuck to the roof of her mouth.

What was the matter with her? Why was her mind wandering in this direction? It wasn't like her to focus in on the opposite sex like this.

She reached for the sweetened iced tea and drank half the contents of the large frosty glass before she could muster any sort of a meaningful response.

She cleared her throat.

"I've covered bits and pieces of it with Mr. Bennett and Mr. Temboni. Mr. Biozzo accompanied me on a couple of the routes further inland," she managed, quite calmly, she was sure. "But no, mostly I've relied on the two Brazilians to help confirm what your two representatives have drawn up. I doubled-checked their information with maps and other documentation provided by the Brazilian government and GlennCorp before reaching my conclusions. It was well researched."

"Your report this afternoon seemed appropriate enough..."

"Seemed appropriate?" Holly leaned forward, fork in hand, the heat rising up her neck. "Seemed appropriate? It was right on!"

Saved from embarrassing herself before she said or did anything she might regret, like throwing her tea in his face, the waitress arrived to remove their appetizer dishes, replacing them with steaming entrees. The aroma of seasoned chicken covered with white wine sauce had Holly's taste buds salivating and, thankfully, her nerves back under control.

Until Jake continued.

"I'm sure you feel your prepared speech was convincing. However, I've been sent down by Mr. Holmes, president of GlennCorp, to personally double-check certain routes before I sign the contracts on his behalf."

"I know who Mr. Holmes is."

"I plan to cover as much of the pipeline route as possible in the next two days," he continued.

"You don't trust your own people?"

"I didn't say that. But, it never hurts to be sure things are in order on such a big project."

"So you came down to check up on them?"

"You might say that. I'm here to do a spot check. The *Vale do Javari* seems like a good place to start."

"Great. I'll go with you."

"Excuse, me?"

Apparently Jake Daniels was also surprised to hear her utter those words.

"I'll go with you," she found herself confirming more emphatically. "After all, I've already covered most of the routes closer to Manaus. This will give me a chance to check out the interior routes further inland as well. How hard can it be?"

The silence that followed gave Holly time to regroup and realize just what she was getting herself into—two days in the rainforest, close up and personal with Mr. 'Sinfully Handsome' Jake Daniels.

Dear, Lord. She'd be spending at least one night out there with him.

In the rainforest. Alone.

She looked across the table. The flickering flame from the candle in the middle of the table danced in his eyes. His lopsided grin told her he was aware of what she had just agreed to, and the fact that she was having second thoughts.

Normally a level-headed, think-before-you-speak person, once again Holly's voice seemed to have developed a mind of its own. She was going to have to be extremely careful and think before she opened her mouth in the future.

Especially around Jake Daniels.

Of course she was going to have to decline the challenge she recognized in his eyes just before his lids lowered, shadowing his thoughts.

Damn, it made him look even more sexy.

His smile disappeared.

"If you think you're up to it, I can make the necessary arrangements. One more person tagging along won't make a difference. Pack light, and don't forget your toothbrush."

"Toothbrush?"

The implication of packing a toothbrush wasn't lost on her. Holly's chin jutted out at the dare.

"Of course *'I'm up to it'.* I have no qualms about hiking into the rainforest, Mr. Daniels."

"*Jake.*"

"*Jake.* Just because I'm a woman doesn't mean I have to have a caravan to lug my belongings around for me. I do know how to pack light. Tell me where, exactly, should I, and my *toothbrush,* meet you tomorrow?"

Holly tapped her foot under the table. The man had the nerve to think she wasn't up to the challenge. That she didn't know how to pack for an overnight trip into the jungle? Huh! She'd show him. What was it her mother always said? Something about keeping the enemy close? Well, why not. He wasn't exactly the enemy, but she did want to find out what he was looking for out there, and she had time to kill before he decided to sign those contracts. This way she could find out what he was up to and prove to him at the same time that her report was right on!

His right eyebrow rose ever so slightly. His lips curled upward as well.

Damn, he was handsome!

"As long as we'll be traveling together over the next couple days, why don't we get to know each other a little better tonight? I hear there's a full moon on the rise, should be a great night for a boat ride. Care to join me?"

She sighed. "Sure." She told herself she was just being practical. It would give her a chance to figure out how to get herself out of this pickle she'd just gotten herself into and still save face. And if she couldn't disentangle herself from going on this expedition with him, she could at least find out more about what Jake Daniels was up to before she did go traipsing into the jungle with him.

Lord, did any of her thoughts make any sense?

She looked back up into Jake's challenging, dreamy Caribbean eyes and nodded her head in agreement.

"Great." His smile widened. "Make sure you wear something warm. The nights can be chilly out on the water once the sun goes down."

****

Music from the local bars lining the main dock of Manaus harbor echoed into the night like a faint breeze. The loud grinding of the water-taxi's motor muffled the sound as they left the wharf behind. Sparkling lights and party-goers faded into the background. Up ahead, Holly gazed at the blazing shades of orange as the sun set over the Amazonian jungle rivaling the hues of a Serengeti evening sky. She blocked out the noise of the boat's motor, her visual senses on overload.

The boat slipped over the Rio Negro to the slow, mud-filled Amazon. Loose, floating debris and water-hibiscus surfed lazily in the evening shadows. Holly leaned against the cool, wooden railing, oblivious to the other passengers as she drank in the ambiance of the warm, tropical night and the enchantment of the evening.

Even though she'd been in Manaus for the past few months, she hadn't had a chance to relax and enjoy herself. The excitement of being in the middle of the Amazon, in the middle of the world's largest rainforest, with tropical breezes literally blowing through her hair, was a welcome respite from the many torrential downpours she'd gotten caught in while checking out the pipeline route.

But she really hadn't minded the weather. This was a job, not a vacation. Thankfully, the project was at an end. She had only to wait for Jake Daniels to do whatever it was he was about to do in checking out the proposed route.

And sign contracts.

Then she'd be going home.

So why not relax and enjoy herself for a change?

Jake Daniels. The man standing next to her definitely had something to do with the enchantment, and the excitement of the evening. In fact, Mr. Sinfully Handsome was standing much too close, his arm touching hers as they both leaned over the railing and gazed at the tropical sunset. She felt a strong pull toward him and wondered if he felt it too.

Crimson swirls mingled with the varying shades of orange as the last rays of the sun's orb disappeared out of sight. Still warm after the heat of the day, the lack of sunshine cooled the earth by steady degrees, the coolness more pronounced now, as Jake had mentioned it might. The breeze off the

Amazon Connection

river cooler than before, Holly shivered.

"Here, put this on." Jake took his lightweight jacket off and wrapped it over her shoulders. "You should've brought a sweater."

"I thought long sleeves would suffice." She was thankful she had worn slacks and sneakers.

The scent of him swirled around her as she snuggled into his jacket. She stepped away from him as if that would help, but his scent was on his jacket. And it clung to her.

It was somehow comforting.

"Thanks," she said. "Where are we headed?"

She looked back out at the tree-lined shore as it drew near. The boat shifted and entered a narrow channel, a flooded marshland, where the tops of high bushes and low trees swayed gently in the boat's wake.

"I thought something touristy would be fun. Something relaxing. We're headed for Lake January. There's a camp there where we can pick up a smaller boat that will take us deeper into the lake system. There are no clouds for a change so we should have plenty of light. After the spectacular sunset, I'm sure you'll enjoy the effects of a full moon."

Holly looked up to confirm his prediction. Sure enough, a full moon was already visible in the evening sky. The spectacular colors of moments before had fully disappeared.

"You sound as if you've done this before."

He nodded. "Once. A long time ago, but not under such inviting circumstance."

His comment reminded her of one of Harold Bennett's remarks about watching out for Jake Daniels being all over her like hot fudge on a sundae. She wasn't ready to be anybody's sundae.

Hot fudge or otherwise.

No matter how enticing Jake Daniels was, she wasn't going there.

15

Think Tony. Think Tony.

The taxi-boat continued to slowly motor deep into the back of beyond as the moon rose over the rainforest and shone down on them like a beacon lighting their way. An hour later they pulled into a small make-shift dock hidden among the heavily wooded jungle. A trail of kerosene lanterns lit the pebbled walkway that led to a thatched-roofed, open pavilion-type hut where they were greeted with typical tropical gaiety. They were led down the romantic path and Holly warmed to the experience and smiled up at Jake. She caught a deep smoldering look in his eyes only to have it quickly shut down behind lowered lids. She stumbled, tripping into the small, flat, narrow wooden boat waiting to take them farther into the night. Jake caught her, his touch unnerving.

Or was it the fact that the boat held only eight people at sardine-tight quarters with flat seats mere inches above the dark lake water that had her trembling?

Her smile faded.

This was starting to push her comfort level. The small boat that had taken her into the flooded woodlands to check out several of the nearby areas where the pipeline was slated to run was more secure then this waterlogged excuse for a floating device.

Seated two by two, elbow to elbow, with Jake's body pressed up against hers proved to be anything but relaxing. Sitting shoulder to shoulder, thigh to thigh with him had tingling sensations coursing through her entire body.

"Did I mention this was a hunting expedition?" Jake asked close to her ear, his warm breath causing the loose tendrils of her hair to tickle her neck.

"*Hunting?* For what?"

"Alligators."

Amazon Connection

"What! Alligators!" Holly jumped up, rocking the flat boat and bumping into a couple trying to board. Jake grabbed her arm, pulling her back down next to him. The boat rocked back and forth, then steadied.

"This is a joke, right?" she hissed in his ear. She didn't want to know the answer. No way was she intentionally going out hunting for reptiles in the middle of the night.

"Nope. No joke. Come on, it's perfectly safe."

"Right!"

Before she could disentangle herself from his strong hold and step out of the boat, everyone was seated and the boat was pushed away from shore. The small motor kicked in and they were off.

They were taken deeper into the night with only the miniscule light from their guide's miner-type hard-hats to shine the way. Hunting alligators at night in the back of beyond was not her idea of a good time, let alone a relaxing one. The romantic feel of the evening ended when Holly turned to discover that their "captain" operating the motor from the back of their floating crate was only eight or nine years old.

The evening was definitely going downhill—fast!

She was ready to strangle Jake Daniels as they continued to weave in and out of glistening fields of white, water hibiscus floating on the surface of the ebony lake, the sweetness of the lovely flowers lifted on the nighttime breeze. Holly's heart beat erratically. The beauty of it be damned! She wanted out.

"They're looking for ruby eyes glowing in the night," Jake breathed in her ear so she could hear him over the roar of the motor. It somehow sounded exotic, a bit erotic coming from his lips. She shivered despite the warmth of his jacket surrounding her as his breath fanned her neck behind her ear.

She didn't want to think of Jake Daniels' lips so

close to her neck. She turned to him with raised eyebrows. He was much too close. Their lips mere inches from each other.

"Ruby eyes!" she gasped.

"The lights on our guide's hats. They shine the light into the reeds and hibiscus to search for alligators. The light mesmerizes them so they're easy to snatch out of the water."

She didn't care about ruby eyes. She didn't care about the white moon glistening off the water and flowers like sparkling snow atop a sun-drenched glacier. The thought of snatching alligators out of the water into the boat had a stranglehold on her emotions.

Why of all places did Jake feel the need to bring her here in order to "get to know her better?" Her ideal date to find out more about a person was not hunting alligators inches above the water in a floating coffin. In fact, the whole experience didn't come close to what had promised to be the start of a wonderfully romantic evening.

Romance, huh! In her dreams!

What had she expected?

She wasn't sure she wanted to answer that question.

If it wasn't for the loudness of the boat's small motor coughing as if it had a bad smoking habit, she'd demand to know what he was thinking bringing her out here to hunt reptiles. Instead, she counted to ten, took several deep, calming breaths, and prayed that luck would prevail and they wouldn't spot red eyes glaring back at them. There was no room to bring another passenger aboard, especially a wreathing reptile with a long tail, lots of sharp teeth and extra strong jaws.

The boat suddenly veered into another field covered with a thick growth of hibiscus. The heady fragrance filled the air. Holly breathed in deeply

Amazon Connection

trying to calm her tattered nerves. As she exhaled, the motor took one last cough.

And died.

Carol Henry

Chapter Two

Careful to keep her hands from dangling over the side of the boat, Holly turned to Jake. His eyes dark as the night, sparkled back at her from the bright moonlight. But it was the devilish grin on his handsome face that had her taking note. That and the fact that their young "captain", whom she spotted from the corner of her eye as she'd turned to Jake, had just pulled the propellers out of the water.

Good, God! They were a tangled mess of long, strong-looking roots that resembled knotted snakes.

Speechless, she looked back up at Jake. He must have seen the panic setting in because he quickly turned to see what had upset her.

"Don't worry," he calmly stated as if they were on dry land and mere feet from the hotel. "He'll have them untangled in nothing flat. Relax. We'll be on our way in no time. Listen to the soothing quiet of the night."

The cacophony of the night life in the surrounding rainforest was anything but soothing. The nocturnal creatures were alive and well and kicking up a clatter—regular party animals. Not to mention the insects buzzing and clacking.

What was this man thinking? The racket, louder than the motor when running, drowned out her thoughts of how she would love to strangle Jake Daniels.

She looked around to see the reaction of the other passengers. To her utter amazement, they were enthralled, excited, and loving every minute of it. Was she the only sane person aboard? The only one to realize what trouble they were in?

Apparently so.

Loud splashing drew her attention back to the front of the boat.

Oh, Lord. The ruby-eyed alligator!

Holly wrapped her arm though Jake's and drew him near.

"What's wrong?" He asked, a hint of laughter in his voice.

"What's wrong?" she hissed in his ear. She couldn't believe he had to ask. "I'll tell you what's wrong. What the hell are we doing out here, Mr. Daniels? Are you trying to give me a heart attack? For your information, this is not relaxing. How can anyone relax hunting alligators in the middle of nowhere. In the middle of the night?"

Jake turned away from her. When he looked back, his gaze was guarded, the smile gone.

"I can't believe you're afraid of a harmless mesmerized alligator. Shining the light in their eyes calms them so they can be lifted by the scruff of the neck without a fight."

"*Scruff of their Neck!* Do they even have a neck? You make it sound as if they're lovable puppies."

"I assure you, there is no threat to us, otherwise they wouldn't bring tourists out by the boatload to experience this exciting adventure. I can't believe you're letting this upset you after all the traipsing you've been doing in the jungle the last few months."

Thankfully, the other passengers were totally engrossed in the proceedings at the front of the boat and weren't paying any attention to their conversation. She felt foolish enough as it was.

"Don't kid yourself. I'm not afraid." The lie tripped out of her mouth as if it were the truth. She could see he doubted her, but she wasn't about to cave into those doubts. "I was startled, that's all. I hadn't expected this to happen, what with the motor giving out like that and the thrashing reptile at the same time. What did you expect?"

"Well, you're the one who wants to follow me into the jungle where we're bound to meet up with a reptile or two now and then. Not to mention a few snakes, some pretty big spiders, and other large wild animals. I thought you'd be immune to such things by now. I can't believe you haven't run across a few of them already while you were doing your 'research'."

Holly hadn't. But that was beside the point. She suddenly realized what he was trying to do, and damn him, it had almost worked. Almost. Although, she had to admit that the thought of traipsing in the jungle with Jake Daniels for two days and one night was daunting in itself. She hadn't thought much about the wildlife that would be surrounding them the entire time.

"If you think you're going to dissuade me from going with you into the rainforest by bringing me out here to the back of beyond and scaring the b'jeepers out of me, then you're mistaken. I'm not the wimp you seem to think I am."

Which was a total lie.

Jake Daniels saw straight though her—no crystal ball needed. She *was* a wimp, especially when it came to things that went bump in the night, but she wasn't going to let that stop her now.

"You've proved your point, Mr. Daniels. I'd appreciate it if you'd take me back to the hotel now."

She felt defeated.

She wanted to wipe the I-just-won-this-round grin that he didn't bother to hide off his face. He either didn't recognize humiliation when he saw it, or he simply didn't care that he'd made a fool of her. It was obvious that he had been testing her.

From an early age she'd been afraid of thunder

and lightening and had hidden under her bed during major storms more times than she could remember. Her mother had found her huddled there with a blanket over her head numerous times and had tried to console her, but it never worked.

She'd tried to work through her fears by getting involved in nature projects in high school. Even tried summer camp a couple of times, but that didn't work either. She had a hard time with all the creepy-crawlies, including being skittish about anything possibly touching her when swimming in the lake with the other kids.

Then, fighting her fears big time, she decided to major in environmental sciences, and ended up working for Wild and Wonderful after she graduated from college. She figured her respect and pseudo-interest in the great outdoors could be handled at a distance. She hadn't counted on actually having to go deep into a rainforest. Short forays on the outskirts were one thing, but overnight in the deep, dark netherlands of a jungle where heaven only knew what was lurking...

There had been no way she could tell Helen she wasn't up to wandering around in the back of beyond. And thankfully it had been a snap so far. But her fears had followed her. She'd always been able to keep them locked inside. Until tonight. And unfortunately, she'd let her guard down, lulled by the beauty of her surroundings. And even worse, it had to be Jake Daniels who had just brought those fears out for all the world to see.

Raw, bruised, vulnerable.

And on display.

"Just as soon as our young 'captain' gets the propellers untangled we'll navigate back to where we started. Should take us, oh, I don't know, a few more hours before we get back to Manaus."

Speechless, she tried to control her inner

23

turmoil. Pushing him overboard came to mind.

"Sit back and relax. Enjoy the night."

Those piranhas swimming below would have him picked clean in seconds. It would serve him right for playing such a dirty trick on her.

Disconcerted to find that her arm still clutched his, she pulled away.

He tightened his grip, pulling her closer instead.

"Sit still. You don't want to tip the entire boat over, do you?"

A loud splash and the sway of the boat had Holly clinging even more tightly. She thought she heard him say something to the effect that he was going to enjoy their adventures in the jungle, but she wasn't certain as the oohs and aahs from the other tourists alerted her to the fact that an alligator was about to join them on board.

Surely it was only for show, and they would put it back in the water—a catch and release tactic as a crowd pleaser.

No such luck.

The reptile, which thankfully wasn't so long after all, was held snuggly in its captor's hand, then settled in his cohort's lap for safe keeping.

Holly's insides started shaking. *Would this night never end?*

The motor suddenly revved up, and without much fuss they were spirited out of the hibiscus patch, speeding back to camp.

Twenty minutes later they rounded a cove blanketed in silvery hibiscus. Despite the beauty of the sight before her, Holly breathed a sigh of relief when she spotted the moonlit outline of the tourist hut up ahead. As soon as the boat pulled to shore, she quickly jumped out, more than ready to head back to the hotel.

Holly rushed inside the hut leaving Jake to fend for himself. She leaned against a table displayed with native handicrafts and took a few minutes to breathe in and out rhythmically in an effort to calm her frayed nerves while the others disembarked. Finally, thinking she had herself under control, she turned to admire the colorful crafts laid out for the tourists. She spied a large plastic-looking beetle the size of her palm. It would make a great gift as a paperweight for her future brother-in-law. Stretching across the flimsy table, making it rock slightly, the paperweight's legs started moving and it scurried across the table and over the side, disappearing into the night.

Holly turned and almost swallowed her tongue as a long boa was being unfurled with flourish in the middle of the pavilion. She circled behind the group as their native host assured them that the snake was "sleepy", and wouldn't harm anyone. She wasn't about to stick around to find out. She'd had enough. She turned to head back to the water-taxi only to have a young native girl sporting another snake block her path. Eye to eye with the writhing serpent, a baby anaconda coiled around the dark-eyed girl's small hand, Holly knew how those poor alligators had felt earlier.

Holly pulled herself out of the trance and looked up. Straight into Jake Daniels' eyes.

And his wide grin.

Damn him! Sending him what she hoped was a razor-edged glare, she side-stepped the snake and high-tailed it back to the boat.

No way in hell was she following this man into the jungle.

No way!

Jake followed Holly at a slower pace. He could tell by the look in her lovely emerald eyes that she wanted to strangle him. He'd given her a good fright which proved his suspicions correct. She hadn't faced half the dangers of the jungle—day or night—while she'd been down here for three months. And she hadn't given them a thought until now. Despite her glare that told him she wasn't backing down, he hoped she'd be too frightened to follow him into the jungle to check out the route Bennett and Grapley had mapped out.

A tinge of remorse washed over him. But it was for her own good. And his. He didn't need someone tagging along, holding him back. He wanted to get in, get out, and head up to Alaska to go fishing. If it hadn't been for his boss's wife about to deliver their first child, that's where he'd be now. Casting off up at Ship Creek in Anchorage.

Jake climbed on board the taxi-boat, his thoughts going back to his conversation with Derrick.

"No easy way to put this, Jake," Derrick had said. "I'm sending you to Brazil. You'll have to postpone your fishing trip."

Jake hadn't been happy about that. As GlennCorp's major trouble-shooter, he'd just come off a job on one of their oil rigs off the coast of Texas. He'd also ended up with a bum shoulder after a scuffle with an angry mob that he'd had to pacify. He rubbed his sore shoulder now just thinking about it. He'd been looking forward to relaxing up in Anchorage; the thought of fresh, pan-fried fish over an open fire had been calling to him for months.

He couldn't remember how long it'd been since he'd had a break. Even his love life was practically non-existent since he'd started working for GlennCorp two years ago. He'd been on call 24/7 for so long now he forgot what it was like to take a lady out on a real date.

The image of Holly Newman and his reaction to her sprang to mind. It was obvious the attraction was mutual. And it might be interesting to see where that attraction might lead. Unless she was involved in Bennett and Grapley's scheme.

"I need you to go down there and find out what's going on," Derrick had told him. "I suspect our two hot-shot engineers are working a money-laundering scheme. I'm not sure this is the first time either. They've been in on the pipeline project from the ground up. They certainly have the opportunity to pull it off. I did some digging and found a few discrepancies to support my suspicions."

Jake had told Derrick to pull the plug on the two, but Derrick had refused.

"What I need is for you to fly down and investigate the situation. I can't afford to start over with the Brazilians. I've put too much time and money into this project to pull out now. Go down there, check out the route they've laid out, and make sure everything is on the up and up. If it isn't, nail those two bastards."

Jake wasn't surprised when Derrick had told him that he'd already arranged for guides to escort him into the jungle to meet with a Dr. Sanchez, a researcher who would help verify a major portion of the route deep in the interior.

"We have a representative from Wild and Wonderful on board down there," Derrick had continued. "She's there at our suggestion to make sure we aren't endangering the wildlife. I want you to keep an eye on her. She could be working with Bennett and Grapley. I found her name and an account number on Grapley's computer files. Even if she isn't," Derrick had told him, "she's been working with them for the entire time and might know something. Get close to her. Check her out."

At the time, Jake had figured it'd be pretty hard for a die-hard, grassroots woman who worked for a company called Wild and Wonderful to cave into giving up her beliefs for a cut in profits. These people were known to be fanatic when it involved saving the rainforest. But then, the amount of money they we're talking about could be an incentive to switch sides. Money was always a big enticement.

Jake had stopped listening to Derrick when he'd told him to "get on the good side of Holly Newman". He'd wondered just what Derrick was asking him to do. He'd pictured Holly Newman as a typical tree-hugger, au natural with hairy legs and underarms.

Now that he'd met Holly Newman, his idea of what a stereotypical tree-hugger looked like had flown out the window. No doubt about it, he'd been blown away by Holly Newman the minute he'd stepped into that conference room. She was nothing at all like he'd envisioned a tree-hugger to be—a middle-aged woman with hair pulled up haphazardly hanging down her back in a careless effort to keep it from flapping back in her face; a face cracked by years of wind and sun damage; long, billowy gypsy skirts flowing down around feet encased in Birkenstocks, and no makeup.

Instead, Holly Newman was slim, young, and beautiful. She couldn't be more than twenty-four, if that. He'd been relieved and appreciative to note that not only were her underarms free of unwanted hair, but that her long, luscious legs were tanned—and hairless! The urge to run his hands over them to discover just how smooth and soft they were had had him stiffening with resolve and turning away from her before he'd made a complete ass of himself. Her makeup was perfect; understated, emphasizing her devilishly sexy green eyes.

And he'd been speechless.

When was the last time he'd been speechless in front of a beautiful woman?

Never.

The image of her long blonde hair swirling around her sexy long neck and shoulders as it shone in the candlelight during dinner earlier, and this evening as it swayed in the evening breeze—he'd wanted to touch it, caress it. And he couldn't help but notice how her blouse had clung tightly against rounded breasts that his hands itched to touch.

Hell, he had to snap out of it. He was on assignment. And he didn't have time for this. For all he knew she was involved in Bennett and Grapley's scheme. He needed to keep reminding himself of that fact. Derrick had told him to *"get close to her, if you know what I mean."* Hell, yes, he knew what his boss had meant. And it hadn't been a hard assignment so far, but he had to focus on the job at hand. And with any luck, he'd have the pipeline route verified by Wednesday afternoon, his investigation completed by Friday, and the Brazilian insider, along with Harold Bennett and Thomas Grapley behind bars, and contracts signed.

With the water-taxi under motion, Jake went in search of Holly. He caught up with her in the lower deck, sitting in the back, almost hidden from sight. The evening breeze from the open window played with her long silky hair.

Jake groaned.

The noise from the motor was louder inside. Conversation was going to be near impossible. He caught her eye, motioning with his thumb that she should follow him up on deck. She ignored him, and turned her head back to the open window.

Damn. The woman had attitude.

Jake wound his way through the passengers sitting in rows of chairs that filled the small area until he reached her side. Without giving her a chance to object, he gripped her wrist and lifted her, with case, off the seat and onto her feet then proceeded to lead her up the stairs away from the crowd and the noise.

The moon high above cast its glow on the water. The light sparkled magically off the river, the waves from their boat bounced hypnotically.

Jake led her to the same spot they'd occupied earlier. Only then did he let go of her wrist. She rubbed at it making him feel like a bully.

"Sorry."

She looked up at him, puzzled. He'd surprised her. She hadn't expected him to apologize.

"I hope I didn't hurt you. I'm not in to manhandling women. Sometimes I don't know my own strength."

"It's fine," she mumbled, turning from him.

"We need to talk, Holly," he said, then leaned against the railing facing her, his back to the water.

"I don't think there's anything to discuss. After all, you've managed to convince me that you don't want me to go with you on your foray into the rainforest. Case closed."

"I'm glad you understand. But I hope you can answer a few questions for me about your findings before I go."

"I've told you everything I know. It was in my report."

"How well do you know Harold Bennett and Thomas Grapley?"

"I don't."

"Come on, Holly. You've spent a few months with them. You must have developed an opinion by now."

"I'm not terribly fond of them, but they've done their job."

"Did they put up a fuss when you suggested they revamp part of the route?"

"Not that I'm aware of, although it meant more work for them. Like I said before, the Brazilian government was a big help. Luiz Temboni and Paulo Biozzo were instrumental in helping me; they worked more directly with your engineers. Perhaps you should check with them."

"I plan on it."

"Is there a problem with this project, Jake?"

"You tell me." Jake noticed she'd become a bit defensive. Had he rattled her cage? Time would tell.

"What's that suppose to mean?"

"Forget it. It probably doesn't concern you anyway." He hoped it didn't. She was either very good at hiding the fact that she was involved, or she really didn't know what was going on. In any case, he'd probably said too much already.

Holly wasn't sure what he wanted to know, but whatever was going on, she wanted no part of it. He might be sinfully handsome, but the guy was turning out to be a jerk. In fact, he was worse than Tony. Tony hadn't tried to demoralize her in front of a boatload of people by scaring her half to death just to prove a point.

For some reason Jake Daniels brought out the worst in her, and she wasn't sure she liked it. She wasn't one to accept challenges that were literally thrown at her feet. But she'd accepted his.

Twice. No. Make that three times. All in one day!

She'd accepted a dinner date. She'd accepted a midnight boat ride. And she'd insisted she follow him into the jungle.

Chapter Three

Holly strolled down the noisy, floating dock of Manaus' harbor at six-thirty the following morning. The warm tropical air felt refreshing after her sleepless night; the sun peeking through the early morning mist.

Chaos met her as she walked along the causeway—trucks filled with pallets of Coca-Cola® squealed and honked as they headed into the city; smaller farm trucks brimmed with bananas, Brazil nuts, and manioc headed toward the cargo ships for export; vendors shouted at each other as they set up their booths for the day. The narrow walkway transformed into a multitude of colorful and exotic wares right before her eyes. The aroma of fresh produce and baked goods mingled with the heaviness of diesel, exhaust, and river debris floating against the pillions supporting the dock.

A warm whiff of tantalizing pastries drew Holly to a stall on her left. Exchanging a few *cruzeiro nôvo* for a pastry, Holly bit into flaky crust, the unknown spice awakening her taste buds. She licked her fingers in delight, savoring the flavor before moving on to look for Jake and the water-taxi that would take them up the Amazon to their first destination.

He hadn't believed she was serious when they'd disembarked from their midnight adventure early this morning that she fully intended to go with him to check the pipeline route. The man was hiding something and she was determined to find out just what it was, even if she had to follow him to the ends of the earth.

Holly looked toward the end of the wharf and wondered how she'd missed the mid-sized cruise ship settled along the dock.

Holly turned back to the wharf to look for her "ship" only to discover at least thirty identical water-taxis moored along the dock, side by side. Jake hadn't indicated a specific water-taxi, and she hadn't thought to ask. She turned to her left and spotted at least ten more double-decker boats bobbing in the water with smaller fishing boats wedged in between.

Passengers from the cruise ship suddenly streamed down the gangplank headed straight for the row of tour buses lined up like giant amphibians waiting for their morning meal. Vendors lined up to the right of the gangplank loudly hawked their wares. To add to the mass confusion, a calypso band burst into song as a group of colorfully clad dancers strutted down the dock, barefoot and twirling their long billowy skirts.

Drawn into the gaiety of music and the swirling red, white, and green skirts and low-neck white lace tops of the dark skinned, black haired beauties, Holly's plight to find her water taxi was forgotten. Men in tight fitting black pants, red cummerbunds and white long-sleeved, frilly shirts pranced down the floating dock, circled the barefooted women, and threw their hands out in supplication—an altogether sensual invite. Holly found her foot tapping to the music, her heart warming to the steaminess of the dance.

"Very provocative, aren't they?"

She didn't bother to turn to find out who was speaking. Jake's low seductive, gravelly words brushed the tendrils of her hair, sending erotic sensations clear down to her toes. How had he found her in this throng of people?

He was much too close. She closed her eyes and

imagined his arms around her, the two of them swaying seductively to the music. She needed to put distance between them.

Now.

"I've been looking for you," she said, opening her eyes and stepping back as she turned to face him. "Not easy with tourists running all over the place. You never mentioned what boat we'd be on. I was beginning to think you planned to leave without me." On wobbly legs, she stepped around him and looked down the long line of boats bobbing in the water.

Jake took her arm and turned her in the opposite direction, a smile on his face. His touch seared her; she couldn't breathe.

"Follow me," he said, guiding her through the crowd.

Jake had told her to be at the dock at seven o'clock if she still planned to go with him. The more she thought about it during the night, the more convinced she'd become that she needed to go. Never mind she was about to embark on a "walk on the wild side" with all kinds of creepy crawlies waiting for her, it was Jake Daniels she was worried about. How was she going to survive being this close to Mr. Sinfully Handsome without making a complete fool of herself?

It didn't help her resolve any as Jake helped her over the gangplank onto the double-decker water-taxi. Once on board Holly made a mad dash for the steep stairway. She climbed up to the top deck, crossed to the other side and leaned against the gunmetal gray painted, wooden railing. From this vantage point she took in Manaus' busy shoreline. Tall buildings behind the wharf highlighted the progress of time. Crowding had become a problem as the indigenous population had worked their way closer to the export capabilities and a supposed better way of life. Unfortunately, economic conditions hadn't been able to keep up with the boom. Hopefully, the pipeline would help alleviate some of the stress progress had created.

The water taxi's engines roared to life. The boat maneuvered out from between the others and motored down the pier across the *Rio Negro* and into the sluggish waters of the Amazon. In the light of day there was nothing romantic about the thick, brown water carrying backwash from the flooded rainforest floor. Dead leaves, brush, groupings of water hibiscus, and trash floated by unheeded.

The sun rose higher in the sky as they left Manaus behind. Surprisingly, its rays reflected off the muddy sepia-colored water. With plenty of time for reflections of her own, Holly shut out the laughter of the other passengers, most of them Brazilians, her mind focusing on the trip into the rainforest ahead. She was determined to get to the bottom of things and find out what Jake was up to.

"Relax. Everything's set," Jake said, coming up beside her. "We'll meet our first set of guides at the next stop. Should take us a couple of hours to get there, so make yourself comfortable in one of the deck chairs if you want. Our guides will take us by long boat into the flooded forest where we'll meet up with another set of guides who'll take us into the interior. We're headed for Dr. Sanchez' village. I assume you've talked to him at some point?"

"Yes. Briefly. He came to Manaus to confer with the team, but I haven't been to his village."

"What did you think of him?"

"He was helpful. I liked him."

"Did he get along with Bennett and Grapley?"

"I didn't pay much attention, although I don't recall them spending much time together. Harold and Thomas spent most of their time with Mr. Biozzo and Mr. Temboni. Why?"

35

Carol Henry

"As I haven't met him yet, I was interested in your opinion. That's all."

Holly wondered why her opinion suddenly meant so much.

"He met with the delegation three or four times, but didn't spend much time with them. I had a chance to talk to him once, briefly. He was very pleasant."

"Don't take this the wrong way again, but it's a long trek. I hope you'll be able to keep up."

"I'll keep up, Mr. Daniels. You just make sure you don't get us lost." She was pleased to see him tense at her remark, and secretly hoped she would be able to keep up with him.

"Hey, I was an Eagle Scout. I never get lost," he joked.

She watched with avid interest as Jake turned from her, rested his elbows on the side of the railing, and clasped his hands together as if in prayer. If he was praying they wouldn't get lost, she wanted to add her prayers to his. His sudden switch from questioning her to joking with her confused her. She was too tired this morning to play these games.

"I'm serious about getting lost."

"That's what our guides are for, Holly, to keep us from getting lost."

"Glad to hear it. How far is this village, anyway?" Somehow she hadn't expected it to be very far. Did he even know where they were headed?

"Far enough."

That aside, she was still confused as to why Jake felt the need to double-check the route himself. Or, why Derrick Holmes wanted Jake to double-check it. The Brazilians appeared satisfied, and had even accepted the reports along with her recommendation. So why had Jake tried to make it look as if her reports weren't credible?

"Why, Jake? Why did you make it look as if I

36

Amazon Connection

have no jurisdiction on the project at the meeting yesterday by rejecting my recommendations?"

He hesitated, looked at her with a face any poker player would die for, before answering.

"Truth is, Wild and Wonderful was hired by GlennCorp, and regardless of your findings, GlennCorp has the final say. Wild and Wonderful is here as a courtesy to help silence any protest in regards to ruining the rainforest. If we do our job right, there shouldn't be a problem."

Not only did that put her in her place, damn him, but the man was still hiding something. She was sure of it.

"The protesters might be mollified," she agreed. "But I can guarantee it won't last if something isn't right with this project, Jake. You know full well that's why I'm here. To make sure the protestors are kept at bay."

He turned around and faced the river, his gaze settling on the murky waters below. He looked back up at her.

"As you've surmised, there might be a problem. Right now there isn't much to tell. Derrick wants the route double-checked."

He held up his hands when she started to interrupt.

"I know. I know," he said. "Just hear me out. Derrick thinks the two men might be cutting corners. I'm here to make sure everything is on the up and up one last time before I sign off on the project. That's all."

"And you couldn't tell me that earlier because...?" Holly couldn't believe it was that simple. No wonder he'd been asking so many questions about the two men.

"I have no evidence yet to confirm such a scheme, so there is nothing to tell."

"What reason would they have to falsify a map?"

37

she asked. "What do they have to gain? After all, it's GlennCorp's project, and they work for GlennCorp."

He didn't respond.

"Despite what you said earlier, Jake, the Brazilian government accepted the project and the route. After all, they'll be the ones to benefit from this project. As will GlennCorp, of course."

"I can't discuss details with you, Holly. I'm taking a risk discussing this much with you now. I don't know what I was thinking."

That did it. She turned and went to find a seat as far away from Jake Daniels as possible.

An hour later the water-taxi pulled alongside a small wooden dock next to a grass-covered hut. Monkeys swung on thin tree branches as Holly wound her way down a soggy, narrow overgrown path where several small wooden flat boats waited. Their supplies were methodically loaded onto one of the boats. Holly was directed to another boat close by. Carefully stepping in, she climbed over the middle seat and sat at the far end. With the guide sitting in the middle to row, that left the only other seat at the opposite end of the boat for Jake.

No outboard motor this time. Perhaps they didn't have far to go.

Seconds after Jake slipped into his seat the guide pushed the boat from shore, hopped in, and in minutes they entered the flooded rainforest. Shrouded in dense vegetation, the deep-blue sky was no longer visible underneath the canopy of the tall trees. Several spider monkeys swung from branch to branch, tree to tree, following their progress while multicolored macaws flew overhead, cawing noisily.

Overcome by the beauty of her surroundings, Holly drank in the vivid green vegetation, breathed in the clean air as they continued for over an hour, meandering down narrow channels deeper into the rainforest. The tannin-colored water barely rippled as the paddles smoothly stroked silently through the water. She couldn't resist dipping her hand in the cool liquid, then let it trickle between her fingers. Until she spotted one of the largest snakes she'd ever seen slithering toward a grouping of giant lily pads growing in profusion to her right.

Oh, dear Lord. What made me think I had the stamina to handle this adventure?

It was definitely going to be a long two days.

****

"What are they talking about?" Holly called to Jake as the small wooden boat finally drifted toward land. It had been two hours and Holly's numb backside had tired of sitting in the same position for so long. She was ready to plant her feet on land and get the circulation flowing in her legs again.

"You don't want to know," he answered from the other end of the flat boat, confirming her thoughts.

"Of course I want to know," she lied. No way was she going to let him know how nervous she'd become already. Putting a brave face on it, she demanded: "What are they talking about?"

"See those two eyes sticking out of the water over there."

He pointed to her right where a log rested against the trunk of a tree. The large knotted nodes where branches once had been attached suddenly blinked. Holly jumped back in her seat. The boat rocked. Her hands flew to her chest.

"Oh my God, it's an alligator!"

Now would be a good time to stay with the boat and paddle back to Manaus. One look at Jake, however and she changed her mind. She could do this. She *would* do this.

She took a deep breath to steady her racing heart, then counted to ten before looking back up at him. She wanted to wipe the smug grin off his face.

"Don't worry, we'll be safe. The guides are here

Carol Henry

to take care of those minor details. Just watch your step getting out of the boat, the ground is quite muddy here."

Holly stood, steadied her shaking limbs then cautiously stepped out.

The guides unloaded the supplies. Jake stepped out, bent to pick up his backpack, hefted it over his shoulder, then picked up hers and handed it to her.

"It should be a short walk from here. Can you manage your own backpack?"

"Of course I can manage," Holly clipped. "I'm not as helpless as you seem to think." She didn't mean to sound so snappish, but the whole ordeal was beginning to take on a surreal twist.

Holly worked at putting the backpack over her shoulders. Jake, she noted, had no problem slipping into his. Grunts and groans and much splashing behind her had Holly scurrying to catch up to Jake. After putting a fair distance between her and the noise, she turned to see the large-eyed alligator roped, tied and already laying in the boat they'd just vacated. Holly shivered. Even if she wanted to, there was no way she was getting back in that boat now.

She turned back toward Jake, walked past him with resolve, and stopped. *Where was the path? A trail? Markings? Anything?* She turned to her right, then to her left.

Nothing. Now what?

Unwilling to claim defeat, she took a deep breath, her back rigid.

"That's what the guides are for—hacking our way through the jungle."

"I'm okay. I just expected to find a path leading into the rainforest. That's all. I'm fine. Really."

She turned to him then, and the concern on his face melted her heart. She looked around Jake's broad shoulders to see what was keeping the guides. And froze. She had to be seeing things. Actually, the

Amazon Connection

problem was, there was nothing to see.

Jake felt Holly tense. So much for having pacified her a moment ago. Even after last night, he hadn't expected her to cave in so soon. He turned to follow her line of vision in order to see what had her frightened this time. He didn't see a thing. No snakes. No alligators. Nothing dangerous. In fact, the view in front of him was anything but dangerous looking.

The late afternoon sun streamed down through the canopy and sparkled off the flooded interior, the dark shades of the rainforest alive with the hushed sounds of nature. Water lapped against the under story and the freshness of the open air made him want to raise his hands and welcome nature at its best. It wasn't Alaska, but it was pure unadulterated heady stuff.

He looked back at Holly, ready to ask what had her in a tizzy this time. But, then it hit him. He twisted back around to the picture perfect scenery.

"What the hell is going on here?" he muttered.

"They're gone," Holly squeaked, rushing to his side. "Oh, my God, Jake, we're stranded."

Chapter Four

The guides weren't coming back. Where the hell had they gone?

Holly suddenly wrapped herself around him. He pulled her closer. Damn, her body heat sizzled his insides. He stroked her back, feeling the firm lines of her spine and muscles. The front of her didn't feel half bad either. Her body shook in his embrace. Warm, and smelling of wild spices, Holly Newman was all woman.

And in his arms.

Ah, crap! He didn't need this now.

He kneaded her tense shoulders, his own muscles bunched up. Checking out this pipeline route wasn't going to be the piece of cake he'd anticipated.

"The guides aren't coming back, are they?" she hiccupped.

"Come on, Holly. It'll be all right. I'm sure they'll be back any minute." He set her from him and rubbed her arms. He needed to calm her down so he could concentrate. Figure out what to do. "It'll give us a chance to regroup. Make sure we have everything we need for the next couple days. There's a dry spot over there. Let's sit down and wait."

He turned her around and gave her a light shove away from the water's edge. He'd give her a few moments to collect herself before he gave her the bad news.

"I'm sorry. I've never been stranded before. Especially in the middle of a rainforest. I'll be okay

Amazon Connection

in a minute."

Jake watched the emotions race across her delicate face as the panic subsided and resolve set in. He bent over to pick up their gear, then dragged it over to Holly. Together they started going through it.

"How long are we going to sit and wait to be rescued?"

"We aren't. We have quite a hike ahead of us, so I suggest we get started as soon as we lighten our load."

He heard her gasp. Why the hell hadn't he refused to let her come along?

"Is this another one of your scare tactics to make me turn around and go back? If it is, you have a warped sense of humor, because I'm not finding this a bit funny. I'm not going anywhere until you tell me what's going on."

"I wouldn't kid about a thing like this," Jake said, his sense of humor long gone. "Just calm down while I try to figure out where we're headed."

"Calm down? Calm down?"

Damn, she was going to give him attitude again. It was the last thing he needed.

Although holding her again...

"Look, Holly, I don't know what just happened here, but I didn't have anything to do with it. If I had to guess, I'd bet Bennett and Grapley are involved with this...this..."

"Harold and Thomas? Why would you blame this on them? In case you haven't noticed, they weren't in the boat with us."

"It doesn't matter. Right now we need to figure out how we're going to carry all our gear to the next point and hope someone is waiting for us with those damn mules. Barring that, let's hope we run across a few friendly natives with a boat willing to take us back to Manaus."

43

"Next point? How do you know which way to go? Do you see a trail? Because I certainly don't see a trail, Mr. Daniels." Holly twirled in a complete circle, kicking up dead, damp leaves and the smell of decayed earth. She sneezed.

God, he didn't need her hysterics now. They had to get started or it was going to be too dark to see two feet in front of them. A fact he didn't want to bring up.

"We have two machetes. You can carry one in case you need it for protection..."

"Protection? What else is lurking in this jungle that's liable to jump out at us?"

"Do you honestly want to know?"

She didn't answer.

Jake dug in his backpack for his compass. He studied it for a few seconds, then satisfied with the reading, dug in his backpack again. This time he pulled out the map he'd gotten from the head of the Brazilian delegation. Mr. Delgado informed him that it was the final route being discussed at yesterday's meeting.

"At least our missing guides weren't totally heartless, they left our supplies."

"Why wouldn't they?"

"Because, they could have kept the food and water for themselves, or sell it to make a profit."

"Maybe they misunderstood your instructions and they'll come back to check on us?"

"In your dreams, Sweetheart. Trust me, they knew exactly what they were supposed to do."

Jake lifted the large backpack, the tent, a bedroll, and the waterproof dry-bag filled with matches, flashlights, batteries, first aid kit, and food, along with other items he'd deemed necessary, over his shoulders. He waited for Holly to do the same.

The heat of the afternoon was long past soothing and it wasn't going to get any better till evening.

Sweat beaded Jake's forehead and dripped down his temples. He wiped the moisture away with his shirtsleeve. Mosquitoes buzzed around his face. He swatted at them, maiming one and upsetting the others. They did a frantic buzz-dance around his nose and mouth. A sudden quirt of spray covered his face. Too late, he raised his hands to protect himself and ended up sneezing. His eyes stung.

"What the hell do you think you're doing?" he wiped at his face again, the smell of insecticide stinging the inside of his nose; he tasted it on his lips.

"Spraying DEET to chase the bugs away."

"Good God, woman, you're going to blind me, then we'll never find our way out of here alive. Put that damn can down and find me a cloth so I can wash my face and rinse out my eyes."

"Sorry. I was just trying to help."

"Don't try so hard."

Holly pulled a lightweight, cotton tank top and a bottle of water out of her backpack. She twisted the corner of the shirt, poured water on it and handed it to him. Jake tilted his head back and squeezed the shirt, allowing water to pool in his eyes. His long, glistening neck drew her attention. Her mouth went dry. She reached for the water bottle and took a deep swig. Oh Lord, wild life wasn't the only danger out here in the jungle.

Jake blinked, took the bottle from her and finished the remaining water in one long draw. Dazed, Holly automatically took the empty container and her damp shirt from his outstretched hand. Poker face in place, his silence spoke volumes.

She watched him go down on his haunches like a predatory animal. He unfurled a map with a confidence she envied.

"A map? A map is going to lead us out of here?" she ranted, beyond worrying whether or not he was upset with her. "Look around you, Mr. Boy Scout. We could be anywhere. Do you have an 'X' marking the spot on that map? Do you even know where we are?"

All right, so she was getting a little excited, but taking quick deep breaths wasn't going to help get them out of this predicament. Going off into the great unknown did not feel like a sound plan either. She was beyond worrying if Jake thought her a wimp.

"Calm down, Holly. I know what I'm doing. This is GlennCorp's map of the intended pipeline route. We simply follow this and we'll get to our next stop soon enough."

"I don't see any markers saying 'start here'. I say we stay where we are and let them find us."

"No can do." He checked his compass. "We go in that direction."

Holly paced back and forth, her ponytail swinging to match the rhythm of her strides. She felt Jake's gaze on her body; her heart raced.

"Stop looking at me like that."

"Like what?"

Jake knew what she meant, but wasn't about to admit it. For all he knew she was part of Bennett and Grapley's scheme and he had to remember that. But, man, she was one sexy lady. He shook his head. Okay, so it wasn't cool to be thinking how enticing she'd felt in his arms while they were abandoned in the middle of the jungle. So he was scum. He'd have to keep his mind off Holly Newman and on making sure they got to the next point without getting lost.

Easier said than done!

Damn. He needed his head examined. Letting her tag along had been a bad idea.

"Sit down, Holly. You're going to wear yourself out and we haven't gotten started yet."

"What plans do you have to get us out of this

Amazon Connection

one, Indy?"

"Nothing so dramatic. We'll use the compass and follow the map."

"Point A to point B?"

"Exactly. According to this map, if we head east for about a mile, we should come to a Para nut grove. Five miles past that we turn to the left, cross a narrow stream, climb a small embankment and we should be at our campsite where our guides will be waiting for us. We'll spend the night there."

"Why weren't they waiting for us here?"

"I didn't make all the arrangements. That was left up to the outfit Derrick hired."

"I think letting Derrick make the arrangements was your first mistake."

Jake figured it wasn't even close to being his first mistake, but he wasn't going to call her on it.

"They were a reputable company."

"Somehow I don't think so. Look, I don't know how long it's going to take to find our 'campsite', but I think we'd better get going. You know as well as I do that once the sun goes down, this rainforest is going to get a lot darker. It's going to be impossible to see where we're going and I already have a feeling we're being watched. And I don't mean by humans."

Jake wasn't so sure about the human part.

He watched Holly bend over and pick up her camping gear. His heart went to his throat—he had to get his mind off Holly Newman's backside if they were going to get very far today.

"I'll carry the tent on the top of my pack," he told her. "We'll split the food between us in case we get separated. We can take turns carrying the waterproof bag."

"Get separated?" she shrieked.

"*In case*. I don't think that's going to happen, but it pays to be prepared."

"Won't all this extra stuff slow us down?"

47

"A bit, but most of the stuff I've sorted out is necessary. Come on, I'll give you a hand with your backpack. You don't want it too loose around your waist or it'll swing back and forth and give you a backache."

"I suspect that won't be the only thing hurting at the end of this day."

She held still while Jake helped her strap the large green sack over her shoulders and around her waist. When he went to tighten it around her middle, she shoved his hands away.

"I can manage this part on my own, thanks. Better get your own gear tied on so we can get started."

"Yes, ma'am," Jake said with a salute, then smiled as he turned away.

Machetes in hand, Jake and Holly cut their way into the dense rainforest, Jake leading the way.

Two hours later, Jake had the feeling they weren't where the map said they were. He also had the feeling they were being followed, and it wasn't because Holly had put that notion in his head. They'd passed the Para nut grove a half hour ago. According to his calculations, and compass, they'd turned in the correct direction. Now, he had the sinking suspicion they should have turned right instead of left. The only stream he could find was on the map.

Crap! They were lost.

Chapter Five

Jake jabbed his machete into the soft earth and slid his backpack off over his tired shoulders. "Are you okay?"

"I'm thirsty, I'm hungry, and I'm tired." Holly let the strap of the pull-along drop, and made a stab at forcing her own machete into the soft earth. It fell with a thud at her side. Stepping over it with a resigned sigh, she realized she'd bitten off way more than she could chew this time. Keeping up with Jake had stretched leg muscles she didn't know she had. They were more than protesting, they were screaming.

The humidity staggering, her body limp from exhaustion, Holly wiped at the moisture beading on her forehead. She didn't bother with the trickle streaming between her breasts toward her navel, her shirt was already sopping wet.

Where was that stream?

She ached to take her hiking boots off and dip her toes in that cool water—if they could only find it.

Trying not to be too obvious, she examined a fallen log to make sure it was free of spiders, ants or other creepy-crawlies. She scanned the area around her. Through the dimming evening light she saw nothing but more lush, dripping wet jungle. The heavy odor of damp earth mingled with the vegetation that spewed pure oxygen into her lungs as she took in a deep breath. In any other circumstance she'd be high on the ambiance, but her body screamed in protest and her mind filled with dread that they had further to go.

Not caring at this point if something was about to jump out at her, she plunked down on the half-rotted tree trunk that looked as if it had fallen over eons ago. Her wobbly legs welcomed the reprieve. She unbuckled her backpack, slid it from her achy shoulders, then bent over to unlace her shoes. She pulled them off and wiggled her toes.

Ahhh, relief.

She'd pushed hard the last few miles. Thankfully she'd just taken her last step for the day.

Her occasional stints at the gym and long walks with her sister hadn't prepared her for this kind of arduous trek. Even the forays she'd taken the last couple of months to check out sections of the pipeline route hadn't been this exhausting. She hadn't realized just how out of shape she'd become since graduating from college. No doubt about it, she needed to work out more. Once she got back home she was going to get serious about an exercise program.

Right after her sister's wedding.

"So? How much further to this stream?" she asked, not wanting to delve into thoughts about the wedding for which she was to be the maid of honor. She rubbed her sore toes through the soft material of her damp sock. "We must be close. We've been hiking forever."

She rubbed her other foot. Yep, blisters were close at hand. She'd die first before admitting as much to Jake. The cool stream would soothe them and she'd be good as new once she got some rest.

Preoccupied with rummaging in his backpack, Holly patiently waited for him to find whatever it was he was searching for. It seemed to take forever.

Her patience ran out.

"Where is that stream, Daniels?" she stated. "Just how much further do we have to hike?"

Amazon Connection

Jake's sharp look met her eyes. She had her answer.

"We're lost, aren't we?" she tried to control her emotions, but the lump in her throat remained lodged there and her voice sounded more like a desperate croak. "There is no stream, is there?"

She didn't want to hear the answer.

"Yes. We're lost, damn it." He admitted, his voice low, angry. "We must have taken the wrong turn. If I had to guess I'd say it's about a mile back. We need to head back to the grove and try again."

"What? No way! That'll take forever. I say we stay here for the night, get an early start in the morning." Holly tried not to sound whiny. Fact was, she was beat, and trekking back to the nut grove on sore feet would be downright grueling. Setting up camp here while there was still a bit of daylight made perfect sense, even though she didn't relish the idea. She told Jake so.

Unfortunately, he didn't agree.

"If the guides are looking for us, they'll check the grove first. That part of the map was correct."

Holly wasn't comforted by the thought of having to trudge back to the nut grove in the growing darkness. "They're guides. They'll find us."

"Hey, I don't like this anymore than you do, Holly. Try to be reasonable." He handed her a foil-wrapped energy bar. "Eat this, then put your shoes back on." He bit into his own chocolate bar. "I agree," he said between chews. "It can get real dark out here. So, the sooner we get started the sooner we'll beat the sunset. I'd rather save our flashlight batteries for when we really need them."

Holly's heart sank.

"I think we should stay here," she insisted, barely tasting the chocolate bar.

"If we go now, we can follow our trail back. It won't take long if we don't dawdle."

51

"Dawdle?" Holly snapped, beyond reason. "You think I've been dawdling? I've been sitting for three whole minutes, for heaven's sake. You can hardly call that dawdling."

Bending over, Holly tried to slip her sore feet back into her boots. She cringed. Damn, either her feet were swollen, or her shoes had literally shrunk. She finally managed to squeeze her feet into them, swallowing a groan of pain.

"Fine," she mumbled to herself when he didn't reply. "But we're staying at that grove tonight no matter what!"

With determination, she hefted her backpack onto achy shoulders and hips, tugged on the make-shift bag with her left hand and grabbed the machete. If she pushed herself, kept up with Jake, and controlled her breathing, and her stride, they should be back to the grove in half an hour. Okay, maybe an hour; it wasn't exactly solid pavement on a level playing field. There was a lot of ground to cover; ground covered with nature's debris. And it wasn't flat or in a straight line. They'd circled many large Kapok tree trunks and if she didn't watch her step, tripping was the biggest hazard.

The deeper they went, the darker it got.

She hoped Jake's feet were suffering as much as hers.

****

Jake watched Holly make her way back toward the path they'd chopped on their way to being lost. He felt like a heel for putting her in danger like this. He'd had no business letting her come with him. No business at all.

As soon as they reached the grove, he'd check the map against the one Bennett and Grapley presented to the Brazilian government and see if he could find what went wrong. Maybe it was a simple matter of going a few degrees off that put them on the wrong path. If those two had intentionally left them stranded, they had a lot to answer for.

It was a pretty sure bet they had.

Jake took another moment to study the map. How the hell did they get lost? And where the hell was that nut grove? They needed to get back on track. "Ah-ha. Follow me," he stated, confident that he had found the problem.

Holly stepped aside to let him lead the way.

"Go ahead, Indy. Just try not to get us lost again."

****

An hour later the sun made its final descent for the evening. They still hadn't reached the nut grove and the nighttime sounds of the rainforest were everywhere. Leaves in the trees rustled as the daytime animals settled in for the night and the nocturnal ones woke for the evening. Birds cawed, monkeys chattered, and large fireflies flashed their signal to their mates. The noisy beetles crunched loudly on forest debris while tree frogs rhibbitted, piercing the evening silence. Bats fluttered hauntingly overhead.

Jake suddenly stopped. He pulled the flashlight from his pocket, and flicked it on the compass to get a reading to verify their position.

Please, let us be on course.

"We couldn't have passed it already," Holly commented, leaning over his shoulder to take a look at the compass as if she knew how to read it.

"We're close." Even to his own ears he didn't sound convincing. His shoulders tense and sore, he knew Holly's must be killing her, too. If he could just find that nut grove he could set up the tent so they could settle in for the night. The guides from the village were sure to find them by morning.

Jake swore under his breath, grabbed the bag from Holly's hands and trudged on. Holly followed closely behind. He was thankful for her silence.

****

Fifteen minutes later Holly's head shot up.

Drumbeats! She swore she heard drumbeats!

Jake, still walking ahead of her, didn't appear to have heard anything. Was it her imagination, or was it the constant buzz that had started droning in her head from the headache that had hit a half hour ago?

Dear God, could she be coming down with jungle fever?

She was tired, but she had to stay alert. There were panthers, anacondas, large insects, bugs and beetles just waiting to pounce at her. Trekking through the rainforest wasn't as romantic a proposition as the movies made it out to be.

The trees overhead rattled. Something cold, slimy, and heavy dropped on top of her head. A blood curdling scream filled her ears. And reverberated clear down to the tips of her toes .

"Get it off!" she screamed. "Get it off before it bites me."

Holly jumped up and down like a pogo stick out of control. She shook her head, but whatever it was refused to let go. The critter clung more tightly the more she tried to shake it free.

"Stop hopping around," Jake ordered as he came to her rescue. "I can't help you if you don't hold still."

"*Just. Get. It. Off. Me!*"

"Turn around and hold still. Let me see what's going on."

"Is it a bat? Oh, God, don't let it be a bat. Anything but a bat. Well, I don't want it to be a snake, either. Just get it off me, Jake. Hurry."

Jake spun her around and shone the light at her head. He gently combed his fingers through the long strands of her damp ponytail.

"That better not be laughter, Daniels. This isn't

funny." She was shaking so hard now she was afraid she was going to wet her pants. And her feet hurt like hell from jumping up and down on her blisters. Not a smart move on her part.

"Just what did you think got tangled in your hair?"

"How do I know? I don't have eyes in the back of my head. Besides, it's too dark to see anything in this god-forsaken jungle." Holly was beyond caring what he thought of her right now. This wasn't a laughing matter.

"Here's the culprit."

Holly heard the humor in his voice as he handed her several broken twigs and a handful of dead, soggy leaves. At first she didn't see anything funny about it. Then she was determined not to let Jake see her smile.

"Thanks," she mumbled, relieved that it wasn't something poisonous ready to eat her alive. She turned from him, clearing her throat. "We'd better keep going."

"Right," his voice light. "Let's keep moving."

Glad that he'd gone ahead of her again, Holly watched his footsteps, keeping her head down, trying to stifle the laughter that was working its way up, ready to escape. She had to be overtired if she thought it humorous.

All right, so maybe it was funny, even though it had scared her half to death.

There! She heard it again.

Drumbeats. Louder this time. Where was it coming from? It surrounded them, making it difficult to tell.

"Jake..."

"Shhhh. I hear it. I smell wood smoke, too."

Holly sniffed the air. She hadn't noticed, but yes, now that he mentioned it, she smelled it too. It was sweet, like incense—rosewood.

At last, they were finally going to be rescued. She plastered herself against Jake's back and hugged him with relief. Jake turned and before she knew it, she was in his arms, her head buried in his chest. She breathed in the maleness of him, a scent headier then the entire Amazonian rainforest. Her hormones went wild. Her weak, wobbly legs gave out just as Jake pulled her close. Did she detect a slight nuzzle on her temple? Oh my, the things it did to her, the tantalizing tingly sensations that were making her weak, her mouth dry.

Overcome by his tenderness, and relief that they were about to be rescued, Holly's resolve steadied. Everything was going to be okay.

Loud grunting, rustling of brush, and stampeding of feet came crashing toward them. Startled, Holly looked over Jake's shoulder at the same time Jake turned, flashlight in hand. Three mid-sized, half-naked Indians were bearing down on them. Heavily painted faces, tattooed bodies with pierced noses and ears were caught in the flashlight's glare. Holly clutched Jake's arm and let out another piercing scream. The buzzing in her head grew louder as it took on the beat of the drums; her heartbeat joined the rhythm. She had to be dreaming—or was it a nightmare? Indians rushed at them, arms waving, their deep, guttural tones menacing.

Four more Amazonian natives leapt from the forest's depths and surrounded them. A heavily painted, fierce-looking male grabbed at her backpack. Holly tugged back. The heavy bag cut loose from her tired fingers and she fell backwards into Jake's arms. Once again she plastered herself to him like a second skin. Her head swam. The stars she saw weren't in the nighttime sky.

"Do something, Indy. You've got to save us."

"Let go, Holly. They're not here to hurt you. Let

them take your bag. Come on, Sweetheart, don't fall apart on me now. We've just been rescued."

Near emotional breakdown, Holly closed her eyes, took a couple of deep breaths and vowed to use every last ounce of energy she possessed to make it through the rest of the night. Either Jake was overly confident, or he was putting on a brave face for her benefit. In either case, it wasn't working.

Jake's strong arms lifted her; he pulled her into his body. She gazed into his eyes, but they were focused elsewhere. She turned to see what held his rapt attention and came face to face with one of the Indians mere inches away. Up close and personal she could see the intricate details of his face paint, the tattoos, his necklaces of bone and feathers. And his beady, dark brown eyes. She turned back into Jake's hold, and shuddered.

"Jake," she whispered into his shoulder.

"Have faith, Holly," he pulled her closer. "These must be the guides sent by Dr. Sanchez."

"They better be or I'll kill you myself."

"If they aren't, you won't have to."

"Is that supposed to make me feel better?"

"Breathe, Holly. Don't pass out on me now. Stay calm."

"Calm? Calm? I don't know who's shaking more, you or me."

"It's not a contest. I'm not denying I was startled at first, but your scream didn't help."

It didn't matter. They were totally at the mercy of these strange-looking people. A shade of darkness Holly had never seen before washed over her. She slipped into oblivion in Jake's strong, secure arms.

Chapter Six

Son-of-a-bitch.

Harold Bennett crouched behind the large roots of a Kapok tree. If it wasn't for Jake Daniels, he wouldn't be in this god-forsaken sweatbox. The only good thing about the damp, moist ground and the constant drip of the humidity falling through the trees was that it muffled the sound of his presence. Thanks to the guides he'd bribed, he'd been able to follow Daniels and that damn, nosy Newman broad all afternoon without being detected. He hadn't anticipated having to deal with her, too.

His plan to reach the village and Dr. Sanchez ahead of Daniels had just backfired. He turned back undercover of the jungle. He hadn't expected Daniels to retrace his steps back to the grove tonight. No matter. Once the tribe settled for the night, he'd have Tracker and the other guides nab the mules and they'd be on their way.

Beads of perspiration formed on his forehead as fast as he could wipe them off. He sucked in air, heavy with humidity, as he concentrated hard to put one foot in front of the other. His mud-covered shoes had lost their shine hours ago. Bennett pulled at his shirt, the last of the buttons popping off with a loud snap, releasing the constriction around his neck. It had little effect.

Damn, even the nights were humid here!

Bennett's confidence teetered on whether he could trust his current guides. He wasn't happy with the turn of events, even though he'd taken great

Amazon Connection

pleasure in watching Holly Newman's reaction to what she assumed was her capture, not rescue. Served her right for interfering. Even Daniels had shown fear, albeit momentarily. What satisfaction it was to witness the scene before him, thanks to the glow from the campfire behind them.

Bennett took one last look at the activity on the other side of the trees. Daniels' rescuers put more wood on the already roaring fire. Damn him. Daniels was not going to get in his way this time. He'd worked too hard to cover his tracks just to have everything fall apart now.

****

Holly opened her eyes, sat up slowly, and gasped. An entire tribe of Amazonian natives were dancing around a glowing bonfire in the center of a large clearing. "Jake," she whispered, her throat parched. "We've got to get out of here. Look at them. My God, they're doing a war dance."

Jake reached her side as she tried to stand. Her legs were as limp as her shoe strings and she was glad for his support.

"They're not doing a war dance, Holly. They're putting wood on the fire," his voice was even, low, and reassuring. "Relax, Sweetheart, everything's okay."

Still lightheaded and dazed by her ordeal, she quietly watched the scene unfold in front of her. Sparks rose from the flames into the deep ebony overcast sky. The flickering flames cast an eerie hue, glistening against the dark, painted skins of the half-naked indigenous people now circling the roaring fire. A scene that she wouldn't soon erase from her memory. She only hoped she wouldn't have nightmares over it.

"Holly, for God's sake, let go." Jake peeled her hands from around his neck. She hadn't realized she'd had such a strangle hold on him. "I told you these men are here to rescue us, not harm us."

"They don't look friendly."

Still weak from having passed out momentarily, tired, sweaty, hungry, and achy all over, Holly anxiously stepped aside and sat down regardless of what might be lurking nearby. She watched Jake kneel down and removed the tent from its bag. The miniscule two-man, pup-tent popped into position. Jake threw the flap up in invitation. She wanted to wipe the smug smile off his face.

"Not the Ritz, but it'll do," he stated, motioning her to enter. He looked at his handiwork, then back at her, and wiggled his eyebrows. "It's outdoor comfort at its best."

Oh, Lord. Closer quarters than she'd expected. Holly's mind reeled at the vision of her and Jake having to share this sardine-can size space for an entire night. It was nothing more than a crawl space. She'd be safer taking her chances sleeping out in the open!

"There isn't much room, is there?" Holly's brain sizzled with the thought of having to lie next to Mr. Sinfully Handsome all night long.

"Don't worry, you'll be safe. Get some sleep. I'm going back to the fire to talk to our guides."

Holly entered the tent on hands and knees. She stretched out, fully clothed, on her back. She pulled her knees to her chest and unlaced her shoes. She kicked her shoes off, wiggled her aching toes. She'd deal with Jake Daniels tomorrow. She didn't have the strength to deal with him tonight.

Holly shut her eyes and gave in to the sleep her body craved.

****

Jake heaved a sigh of relief that Holly was settled for the night. He walked to the campfire to join the *Kanamari* Indians to find out what the plans were for the following day.

Amazon Connection

The Indians welcomed him as he drew near. Ivan, the chief, informed him that the mules were tied up at the other end of the clearing. Tomorrow they would be escorted further inland to the river. There they would motor upstream for many miles to the village. They apologized if they had frightened the '*ladyzinha*'. It was not their intent.

Jake cringed. If Holly ever got wind that the natives referred to her as "little lady", she'd slay them alive. If he'd learned one thing about her already, it was that she'd worked hard at trying to be brave. He'd seen the disappointment in her emerald eyes each time she'd given in to her fears. He had to give her credit for even tagging along into the dark jungle. She was braver than she realized.

An hour later, Jake entered the tent and stretched out next to Holly, careful not to get too close. He'd watched her crawl into the tent earlier. Her backside sticking up in the air had almost had him following her inside, his concentration on his assignment nearly forgotten.

The woman was dangerous.

He was grateful she was asleep, and that they were no longer floundering around in the rainforest. He steadied his breathing in an effort to relax before closing his eyes. As tired as he was, however, as hard as he tried, sleep eluded him. He'd been in worse situations over the years. Situations that called for short power naps and long stretches without sleep. Keeping alert was key in his line of work. Listening, waiting and watching for any sign of danger had become his way of life. That went for hiking through jungles. If he'd been more alert instead of thinking about Holly, they wouldn't have ended up in this situation.

He wasn't use to worrying about someone else's neck, regardless of how enticing that neck was. He worked better alone. Period. He liked it that way.

61

His wasn't your typical walk-in-the-park kind of job. He didn't put other people in danger; he got them out of danger. So why the heck had he let her talk him into letting her tag along?

Jake found himself inching closer to Holly. Her body heat and womanly scent made his stomach knot and his desire harden. Hell, he had to get his mind off Holly Newman and his own libido back on track. He forced his mind back to the reason they were in the Amazonian jungle to begin with. And the fact that Holly could be involved in Bennett and Grapley's scheme. Regardless of what his instincts, and libido, thought.

He wrestled with the question he couldn't seem to answer. What *were* Grapley and Bennett really up to? Why would they leave them stranded? If he didn't verify the route and get back to sign the contracts by Friday, they wouldn't be able to walk off with a cool million. It didn't make sense.

Why would Bennett or Grapley follow him into the jungle? Neither had the stamina for it; they were both pretty much out of shape, and that was putting it mildly. As for the guides and the boat disappearing? Maybe it had just been a fluke after all.

Maybe he was being too suspicious.

And maybe wild boars flew in pairs.

The droning noises of the nighttime jungle overrode his thoughts. Jake's eyelids closed.

And snapped open.

Holly's warm, sexy body snuggled into his already aroused one. Dear God, he didn't dare move. Her right arm snaked across his middle, and clung to him. Her smooth, tender face turned and nuzzled his chest. He drew in a deep breath, held it, then let it out slow, steady, in an effort to control the burning emotions filling his veins to fever pitch. He didn't want to be feeling this way when it came to Miss

Amazon Connection

Holly Newman. He had no business acting on emotions that sizzled every time he looked at her, let alone got this close.

What had he been thinking?

Jake could tell she was unaware of her actions. He placed his right arm along hers, the touch of her smooth warm skin was like caressing a piece of fine porcelain; he couldn't resist the urge to draw her nearer. She settled into him and his entire body responded shamefully. He smiled, pressed a light kiss to her temple.

Big Mistake.

No way was he going to get involved with this woman. He still hadn't determined if she was mixed up with Bennett and Grapley. And even if she wasn't, his job wasn't conducive to long-term relationships. He worked alone. No diversions to take his focus off his job. He'd already screwed up once, he wasn't about to do it again.

And he didn't figure Holly Newman the type to agree to a one-night stand.

What the hell! He'd worry about all that in the morning. He pressed another kiss to her warm, smooth forehead, this time with more emotion.

****

Holly woke with a start and found her body wrapped firmly around Jake's very warm, very sexy body. Not willing to relinquish the security of being nestled so snuggly in his arms after her wild dream, she clung to him a moment longer before relaxing against him. Vivid thoughts of her dream—*make that nightmare*—flooded her mind. Abandoned deep in the Amazonian rainforest, she'd been surrounded by a tribe of man-eating natives. But in her dream they had carried her to a boiling cauldron, flames licking the sides of the soot-blacken pot.

Boldly painted, near-naked Indians danced in a circle in celebration of their sacrifice to the God of

Hunger. She'd been the sacrifice they'd been cooking up. Eyes from every corner of the jungle peered at her as she was lifted high above the boiling water.

Jake had run forward in a scout uniform followed by a troop of boys in matching uniforms. She'd been ecstatic thinking she was about to be saved. The troops came to attention, saluted her in unison, then watched as she was lowered into the boiling pot. Flames licked higher, grabbing at her legs. The red-orange flames turned into green viper snake tongues hissing, writhing, and lashing in and out trying to reach her. Like magic, the cauldron transformed into a huge kettle drum, while the snakes mystically changed into powder-white bones. The natives used the bones to beat out a chaotic rhythm on the tightly stretched hide. Loud booming beats escalated to fever pitch. Natives danced themselves into a frenzy. The scouts ran off into the night leaving Jake behind. She called out to him, but instead of rescuing her, his words became a chant. "I'm sorry. I'm sorry. I'm sorry." The words faded into the night.

She'd reached out to him.

And he was there.

She opened her eyes to find herself held securely in his arms.

Except for their breathing—Jake's slow and even, hers shallow and rapid—everything was dark and eerily quiet. About to turn away, she changed her mind. What would it hurt to be this close to Jake's warm, protective body for a few more moments? It wasn't as if he knew she was practically lying on top of him. She was fully clothed. So was he. She relaxed, drew comfort from his nearness, closed her eyes, and feeling very safe and secure, went back to sleep.

****

When Holly woke the following morning, Jake

was already gone from the tent. Every bone and muscle in her body ached. Stretching, her hands came in contact with the canvassed ceiling. She was reminded of the limited space inside the tent. She sat up slowly and rubbed at her achy feet and gasped as pain shot through her foot.

She pulled her socks off and winced when she saw the large, red blisters broken and raw. An even larger blister covered the bottom pad of her left foot. An inch in diameter, it still oozed a clear body fluid. She refused to look at the dried blood on her socks; her childhood fear of seeing blood would have her head reeling and her legs shaking.

Holly sent up a silent prayer of thanks for the mules Jake said would carry them and their supplies to the river this morning. She would never be able to put her shoes back on and traipse through the rainforest with her feet in this condition.

She dug in her backpack for a clean pair of socks, the first aid kit, and a few bandages. Padding on the bottom of her left foot would hopefully help ease the discomfort, as well as keep it clean.

About to apply the First Aid Cream, Holly was startled when Jake threw back the tent flap and knelt down beside her.

"Don't you knock?"

"A bit jumpy this morning?" Jake didn't give her a chance to answer. "I noticed the blood on your socks this morning. You must have been in a lot of pain yesterday. Why didn't you say something?"

"I didn't want to slow you down."

"I could have bandaged them so they wouldn't be in such bad shape this morning. Here, give me your feet." He reached for them, clasping his long fingers firmly around an ankle. Deftly, he rubbed ointment onto her blisters.

"Holy Batman, Robin, that stuff smells like bat dung. Are you sure it's sanitary?" Holly wrinkled her nose.

"Ivan gave me ointment for your blisters. I've been assured it won't hurt a bit. It's nature's pain killer. The basis of it comes from *Euphorbiaceae*, part of the poinsettia family. Ivan said it may be a healing ointment, but it can also blind you, so keep your hands away from your face if you touch it. You'll be riding one of the mules today so you'll be able to keep off your feet for awhile."

Thank, God!

His touch gentle, the salve immediately soothing. Holly stretched out her other foot willingly regardless of the concoction's smell. Who cared what it smelled like as long as it achieved the desired effect? Past the initial application, however, the circular motion of Jake's thumb as it rubbed hypnotically against her tender skin played havoc with her emotions. Having lain next to him all night long, thinking about how she'd been wrapped around him, had her closing her eyes as she savored the warmth of the moment. And let it linger. When she opened them, Jake was studying her intently. His look confused her. It certainly couldn't be anything more than the reflection of her feelings mirrored in his?

Could it?

"Come on," he said. Clearing his throat he handed her a cup, breaking the spell. "Breakfast is served."

Holly reached for the small bowl-like cup filled with a watered-down looking milky substance. She drew it to her nose. "Yuk. This smells like chalk. I'll have an energy bar instead." She handed the cup back to Jake and reached for her backpack.

"There's a stream on the other side of those trees. You can wash up before we break camp," Jake said, taking the cup from her.

It took Holly longer to hobble on bandaged feet

to the creek then it did to wash up. After washing and relieving herself out of sight of the others, she worked her way back to the clearing. The sky a vivid blue, she was more than ready to face the day ahead. She stepped from the shaded depths of the rainforest and quickly covered her eyes to ward of the brilliance of the morning sun. It took a few seconds for her vision to adjust to the light. Only then did she realize that the entire campsite was already packed and ready to go. It was as if they had never been there.

Holly searched for Jake and found him standing next to several anxious-looking Amazonians. His body language puzzled her; head bowed, legs apart, body taut, his hands held tightly behind his back. Jake seemed to be listening intently to what Ivan and the others were saying. As if sensing her presence, Jake turned in her direction. Their eyes met. Holly's heart stopped, then picked up a rapid rhythm sounding exactly like the drumbeats in her dream. Jake turned his attention back to the guides and the discussion continued.

Now what?

Holly braced herself as Jake swung around and headed toward her. Uh-oh! His poker face was firmly in place. Holly felt the tension sizzle with every step he took. She knew without him uttering a single word that she wasn't going to like the news he was about to share.

Trouble had befallen them once again.

Did trouble always follow him wherever he went?

Chapter Seven

Preparing for the worst, Holly took a deep breath, held it a moment, then let it out slowly. A drop of water dripped from her wet bangs onto the tip of her nose. She reached up to brush it off, shifted her stance to rest more comfortably on her right foot—the one that didn't have a blister the size of Texas on the bottom—and stared Jake down as he came toward her in slow motion.

Her mind buzzed with trepidation. Remnants of her dream still lingered. Scenes from a rerun of *The Good, The Bad, and The Ugly*, one of her father's favorite Clint Eastwood movies, played out in her mind.

Where was a white steed when you needed one?
Might as well meet bad news head on.

Holly put her hands on her hips and walked toward Jake—actually hobbled—to meet him halfway.

"So, Daniels, what kind of a fix have you gotten us into this time? Those guides don't look any too happy about something. In fact, they look pretty darn nervous."

Jake's jaw clenched. She could actually hear his teeth grind.

"This is no time to attribute blame, Holly. If you remember, I did try to talk you out of coming in the first place."

"So, what's wrong? Looks to me as if they're ready to hit the warpath, again. And don't tell me it's my imagination."

"Actually, I had to talk them out of doing just that. They're pretty upset."

"What?" Holly staggered backwards at the implications his words invoked.

He reached out to steady her. She slapped his hands away.

"Just tell me what's going on, Jake. What happened that makes you think they're ready to attack? And who, for God's sake are they aiming for?"

He didn't sugar coat it.

"The mules are missing," he stated, watching her closely. "Someone untied them and took off with them during the night. I'm afraid you'll have to walk to the river along with the rest of us. I'm sorry. I know how painful walking on broken blisters and sore feet can be."

"You don't think I can walk, Daniels?" Holly blustered, reeling from the scare of an actual tribal war. She recovered long enough to thank her lucky stars that their rescuers had turned out to be friendly. And willing to be of service.

"Look, Holly. You don't have to prove anything to me. I know how strong you are. But this is different. We're in the middle of the jungle, and someone has just provoked these people by taking off with valuable merchandise and transportation."

His normally unshakable persona had vanished. That worried her more than anything.

"What do we do now? How long will it take us to get to the river and those boats?"

"I don't know," he answered. "Ivan is sending half the guides to search for the mules; the other guides will stay with us."

He reached into his pocket, pulled out a nutrition bar and handed it to her.

"That *Palom de leche* I gave you to drink earlier is more nutritious and filling than this chocolate bar, but I guess this will have to do. You'll need something to keep up your strength if you're going to be hiking all morning."

"If you're referring to that chalky stuff that smelled like Milk-of-Magnesia, it made me gag just thinking about swallowing it."

"I put it in your canteen."

"You what?" she cried out in disbelief, their dilemma half forgotten.

"For God's sake, Holly, get a grip. These indigenous people have been living off the land for centuries. They know what they're doing."

"Humph." Holly didn't know what else to say. She knew many miracle cures had been discovered in the rainforest, thus her attention to detail and maintaining certain standards in determining the pipeline's route.

Close to starting a lecture about the importance of saving the rainforest, Holly stopped herself before she started—Jake had neatly changed the subject on purpose in order to take her mind off their most recent drawback. No way was she going to let him get away with it.

"Tell me what's going on here, Jake. First we get stranded in the middle of nowhere when our boat and guides go missing. Then we follow a map that leads us further into the back of beyond and get lost. We're practically attacked by wild Indians. And now the mules are missing? Please tell me there really is a village out here somewhere where people are waiting for us. People who actually know we're coming. People who will miss us if we don't show up sometime soon."

"It does look like fate is against us, but Ivan has assured me that we're in safe hands. We aren't lost. And, yes, people are waiting for us and know that we're out here."

"Good, because I'm beginning to believe someone

is plotting against us," Holly said, thinking back to Jake's remarks about Harold Bennett and Thomas Grapley. "Don't tell me you honestly think your field engineers are behind all this? Somehow I have a hard time believing that."

"You're right. Forget I mentioned it. As soon as we get to the village and speak with Dr. Sanchez and verify the maps one way or the other, the sooner we can get out of here."

Thinking about the discussion she'd had with the two men at a restaurant a few days ago, Holly had a deep, uncomfortable feeling that Jake might be right about the two men. She chomped down on the last morsel of her energy bar, chewed, then swallowed. No way could that incident have anything to do with the present situation. Jake was wrong. Harold and Thomas might be a couple of womanizing scumbags, but that didn't mean they were the sort to pull these kinds of stunts. Except for the short forays into the more populated parts of the rainforest, she couldn't picture the two men following them deep into the jungle on purpose.

Holly had all to do not to limp as she walked away from Jake. "Come on Indy, if we're going to make that village anytime soon, we'd better get these guides moving."

She hoped he had more of that god-awful salve in his backpack, her blisters were starting to sting already.

As they approached the guides, Ivan stepped forward, blocking her path, effectively stopping her from joining the others. Holly jumped back.

Now what?

Ivan smiled and reached his hand out to her.

In the daylight Holly could see more clearly the black dots that adorned the bridge of his nose. Wide red lines were smeared carefully across his cheeks. A feather earring hung like a bobber on a fishing line from his elongated right earlobe, and multiple beaded bracelets covered his arm from his wrist to his elbow and sparkled in the morning sun. He didn't look so threatening in the light of day.

"A gift, '*ladyzinha*', for you." Ivan held a two-toned hyacinth-colored feather, intricately painted in his dark, bony hand. It was an exemplary example of Amerindian artwork, and Holly was overwhelmed by his generosity. She smiled and accepted the gift.

She studied the small item closely. When she looked up, the entire tribe was circled around them with silly, crooked smiles spread across each of their sun-burned, boldly painted faces. They didn't look at all threatening today.

"It's beautiful." She smiled, her heart truly filled with appreciation for their kindness. She felt foolish now for the way she had behaved the night before when they had rescued her.

"I do for you." Ivan stepped forward and easily slipped the single earring through her pierced earlobe already holding a golden loop she'd forgotten she was wearing.

"I am honored. *Obrigada*," she said, then bowed. She smiled at each man in turn. "*Obrigada*," she repeated to every one of them.

Ivan turned from her, putting a swift end to the ceremony. He addressed his men. As one, they all headed straight into the rainforest in a comically single-file fashion. Holly followed, her heart overflowing. Such a small gift, it touched her very soul. She felt protected, safe, like being in Jake's arms last night.

She turned toward Jake, and for once his expression wasn't guarded. The look in his eyes told her she'd done the right thing. His approval meant more to her than she cared to admit. She blinked back the tears starting to pool in the corner of her eyes.

Lord, she felt as if she was part of a Hallmark card commercial.

She quickly turned back to follow the guides.

"I'm not married to Ivan now, am I?" she threw over her shoulder to Jake. She heard him chuckle, and kept walking. "I'd better not be."

****

They'd been walking steadily for some time, giving Holly plenty of opportunity to think. Were Harold Bennett and Thomas Grapley really responsible for their dilemma? Why? There had to be a missing piece to the puzzle somewhere. She'd bet her plane ticket back home to New York that Jake Daniels held the errant piece. He was keeping something from her. But what? He'd indicated that the maps were fraudulent. But why would the two engineers go to so much trouble to draw up fake maps to present to the Brazilian government? Certainly the Brazilians would know the difference. Besides, she'd approved those maps. She hadn't found anything wrong with them. Well, at first she did, but then they'd changed them.

The longer she tried to figure it out, the more baffled she became.

With the day wearing on, sunlight streamed hotter through the canopy. It pulled the moisture from the soil and made the air heavy and misty. If not for the shade of the gigantic canopy, their trek would be even more hot and unbearable. With the guides carrying their belongings, including both backpacks, Holly found it less difficult to maintain the slow, yet steady pace, pleased that her feet were numb from the salve Jake had applied again. And that she wasn't slowing everyone down.

At the third rest stop Jake applied more of that awful-smelling poinsettia paste to her blisters. The urge to keep her shoes off and go 'native' was tempting as they hiked through the rugged, but soft terrain. She knew better, however, as her tender soles and pads were no match to those of the toughened ones of the *Kanamari*. They had calloused feet and were oblivious to the sharp, jagged twigs and other dried debris littering the ground.

They traversed steep inclines, crossed shallow running creek beds that in the summer months would otherwise be dry. Back home the creeks would be gurgling with melted winter snow as the clear cold liquid rushed over polished rocks. She longed for the coolness of them now. She'd give anything for a single ice cube. Or a tall refreshing glass of iced tea.

Without thinking, she lifted her canteen and took a deep swallow, then immediately spit it out. She'd forgotten Jake had filled the container with *Palom de leche*. After the initial surprise, however, she realized it didn't taste as bad as she'd anticipated. She took another sip and let it slide down her parched throat. She had to give Jake credit. It didn't taste so bad. And it was filling.

Holly relaxed for the first time since striking out on foot that morning. Her surroundings took on a brighter image of what she considered a rainforest to be all about—it teemed with life. Monkeys swung noisily from branch to branch, colorful birds flitted in and out between the tall trees. The *Kanamari* Indians formed a single line with her and Jake in the center. It reminded her of a National Geographic expedition she'd watched on television. The participants had been roped to each other as they traversed the peaks of a sand dune in the Sahara Desert.

She was glad they weren't tethered together now.

What an adventure this was turning out to be. In reality, each of their mishaps had, thankfully, come to naught. They were safe and there was no

Amazon Connection

reason she shouldn't be taking in the sights and sounds. Life wasn't so bad after all.

Not an alligator or snake in sight!

Ivan suddenly let out a shout. Everyone halted. Like trained soldiers, they recognized the authoritative tone and chill in their leader's voice.

Including Jake who stopped, causing Holly to bump into him, knocking him forward. Jake steadied himself and rushed to Ivan's side.

Holly dogged his heels.

"Stay back," Jake cautioned over his shoulder.

"If something is wrong, I want to know, too."

Reaching Ivan's side at the same time, they both stopped, and looked around. Holly didn't see anything wrong. Ivan stood, almost transfixed. He extended his right arm, pointing it at a freshly snapped sapling that dangled across their path. What did a bent branch have to do with anything? Why had it spooked their guide and the rest of the *Kanamari?*

They stood in silence and scanned the wooded area that surrounded them. Holly craned her neck around Jake's broad shoulders.

Nothing.

"We go back," Ivan called out to them in a loud and authoritative voice. "Stay out. We go around."

"Around?" Holly gasped, checking the area for danger. *What was to go around? And why?*

"We are by *Vale Do Javari.* We go back," Ivan answered her thoughts.

"Jake? How did this happen? We shouldn't be anywhere near this place." Holly looked around again, expecting to see dart-throwing natives circling them. It was a well-known fact that the indigenous people from the *Vale de Javari* were never seen. And if they did make themselves known, you never lived to tell about it. "This area is off limits to even the locals. The *Flecheiros, Tsohom*

75

Djapá and *Korubo* have lived here for centuries without contact with the outside world. I made it clear that this area was not to be disturbed under any circumstances. The route should be as far away from this area as possible. At least thirty miles."

"Exactly. We should be farther north of this region by now, not right next to it," Jake confirmed.

Holly hoped they weren't actually inside the invisible boundaries.

"I don't understand. Why are we so close to this area? Are you sure you have the right map?"

"Unfortunately, I do have the right map. It just isn't the map Bennett and Grapley gave the Brazilian delegation. What do you know about this?"

"Me?"

"Yes. You. You told me you made them change the route. Why?"

"Because it ran too close to this site, as well as two others that were off limits."

Before Jake could respond, Ivan quickly assembled his tribe and led them away from the area leaving her and Jake wondering what had gone wrong. Holly was no longer listening to Jake. If this tribe of natives was turning away because of a simple twist of a sapling in the middle of the jungle next to a forbidden area, then she was going to join their exodus without a fuss. She followed them, not bothering to see if Jake was beside her. She no longer cared about Harold Bennett and Thomas Grapley. She didn't care about the Brazilian government, GlennCorp, Wild and Wonderful, or maps. All she cared about at the moment was that she not end up with a poison dart sticking out of her neck, lying face down on the jungle floor, or being dunked in a boiling cauldron in preparation for the evening meal.

Jake caught up to her. Without breaking stride he put his arm around her waist. He kicked up the

Amazon Connection

pace and dragged her along. Holly didn't protest. She knew it was every man, or woman, for themselves. A supporting hand was more than welcome, Jake's accusing tone forgotten.

On alert now, she panned the area for signs of danger. What she saw had her stomach clenching and her knees knocking. Somewhere along the way the guides had done some hunting. Limp, lifeless wooly monkeys were slung over several shoulders. Holly shuttered. Others totted cumbersome-looking white sacks.

Stark crimson blobs, somehow exotic in the dark jungle light, made her queasy. Telling herself that this was a different culture and that these people survived by living off the land didn't help. The sight of that much blood was the last straw. Her insides protested. She swayed. The damp earth rippled and rose up at her. She couldn't breathe. She stumbled.

"What the...?" Jake turned and caught her more securely to him. "Are you okay? It was just a twig..."

"Blood... I hate blood..."

"Blood?"

"Monkeys. Blood."

"Monkeys? What are you talking about?"

Jake held her still while she shut her eyes and caught her breath.

"They're carrying dead monkeys. God only knows what's in their sacks. Look." She tried to point in their direction, but the sight of all that crimson blood had her head spinning again.

She leaned into him for support. He held her steady, wrapping both arms around her. Dying in his arms at this very moment would be a welcome respite.

"I think we have supper."

"What?"

That did it. Her stomach lurched. She twisted out of his arms and sank to the ground.

77

"You aren't going to be sick are you?"

Too late. Dry heaves ensued.

Jake knelt down to comfort her. Once she had herself back under control he handed her the canteen.

"Here, drink this."

"I couldn't drink another drop of that milky stuff right now."

"It's water. Come on, Holly. Walk it off." He grasped her hand, pulled her upright, and nudged her along, slowly. "Stay behind me and don't look at them. We have a ways to go and if you wimp out now we're never going to get there."

She took a few more steadying breaths and let them out slowly. *I can do this, I can do this,* she chanted. *I can do this.*

Putting one foot in front of the other, together they caught up with their guides. Looking straight ahead Holly forced herself to think of something other than this latest set-back. Unfortunately her thoughts centered in on Jake Daniels and how patient he'd been with her despite his annoyance with her.

Jake Daniels wasn't much of a jerk, after all.

Chapter Eight

Stealing the jackasses in the middle of the night had been a slam-dunk. Tracker had them untied and out of there before anyone knew they were missing. Leaving well ahead of Daniels and the Newman broad would give him plenty of time to make it to the village before they did.

They'd ditched the donkeys at the rivers' edge and were now motoring upstream. Tracker had taken care of the animals. Harold didn't care what happened to them, they had served their purpose and were no longer any use to him.

It took longer than he had expected to go upstream, but he'd been glad for the rest, and the cooling breeze off the river. By the time they finally pulled alongside the village late Thursday afternoon, clouds obliterated the blue sky. A dreary glow hung over the *Juti* River. It was going to rain. Harold didn't know which was worse, the hot sun, the torrential downpour, or the heavy humidity that came afterwards.

A row of thatched roofed, windowless houses, built up off the ground on stilts, lined the shore. Naked children rushed down the muddy bank, curious to get a look at the new arrivals.

Heathens! The lot of them!

Bennett stepped from the boat. His shoes sank into the thick, clinging muck. *Damn-it-to-hell!* He was sick and tired of trying to keep his shoes mud-free. He cringed as he lifted first one and then the other as the soft mud sucked at his feet. He slid,

79

Carol Henry

teetering precariously before righting himself on the short climb up the embankment. Shoes squelched and squeaked with every step.

He hated it out here in this god-forsaken middle of nowhere. He definitely couldn't wait to leave it behind. But it had been worth it so far. It wouldn't be long now before he reached the village and Sanchez.

His breathing labored from the short climb, he turned to speak to Tracker. The damn guide had already climbed back into the boat and was issuing orders for the others to continue up stream as planned. Good. With them out of the way, Daniels would have no indication that he'd been there. Or that the boat would be waiting for him further on up so he could make his escape up-river to Tabatinga and the Colombian border.

Smiling, laughing children holding up their pets rushed toward him. As if he gave a rat's ass. Lizards and sloth were tethered to short ropes. Snakes coiled around small hands. They shoved the docile-looking animals in his face. If he wanted to deal with kids, hell, he would've stayed at home in Hoboken with his own brood.

He pushed his way between the children and continued toward the inner circle of the village. Two young native men dressed in shorts, yellowed tank tops, and covered in tattoos, smiled dirty yellowed smiles and bowed in welcome. He hadn't expected the casual clothing. Progress had evidently reached the village along with Dr. Sanchez' research. Hygiene obviously was still a problem.

"Sanchez?" Bennett asked, wanting to be done with it. "Take me to Sanchez." He wiped his forehead with his arm.

The men pointed behind them, garbling unintelligently, stupid smiles on their ugly pierced faces. Harold dismissed them and headed in the

80

direction they indicated. It was a good thing Sanchez spoke English.

Harold found the ground peaking and leveling out as he wound his way through the village. Houses further away from the river rose up on platforms to accommodate the rise in ground water during the rainy season and to keep pesky creatures out. Chickens clucked, scratched the ground, and nested under several of the make-shift shacks, while pigs rutted under others. The stench from animal droppings mingled with the damp earth and the hot afternoon sun baking down on it all day, permeated the air. His stomach retched. He gagged from the stench. He pulled a handkerchief from his pocket and covered his face.

Across the compound at the edge of the rainforest buildings stood against the backdrop of the jungle. Less crude, these structures were more secure with doors and shutters at the windowless openings. To the left of those sat an oblong pavilion with wooden tables and folding chairs. Blue plastic tablecloths lined the long tables. Harold Bennett headed in that direction.

Harold met several grotesque but smiling Indians pointing toward the pavilion. "Doctor, Doctor" they called as they ran in search of Dr. Sanchez. Harold stepped onto the wooden floorboards, his mud-caked shoes echoing his every foot-fall as he carefully made his way down the center of the open pavilion.

"Ah, Mr. Bennett, what a surprise. Mr. Daniels could not make it, I assume?"

Harold shook Sanchez's hand. The man had a firm grip.

"Sorry. I'm afraid he was detained." Posing as Daniels' replacement was going to be easier than he'd expected. The man didn't have a clue.

"You will join me for a bite to eat?"

"Something to drink would be great. It's been a long day."

"Not to worry. Come. Have a seat."

The two sat across from each other and were immediately waited on by a young Amazonian girl Harold guessed to be in her early teens. They were each presented with bottled water. Harold drank half the contents in one swig, the taste of clear water a treat. Before he knew it, the girl placed a bowl of thick mud-colored soup in front of them. The smell made his stomach lurch and he had a sudden urge to puke. He reached for his handkerchief again.

"It is not much, but it is seasoned and hearty. You must be hungry after your journey here, no?"

It looked like shit and smelled like squash. He hated squash. He knew better than to show discourtesy, however, especially after having just arrived. A lot was riding on him placating the man sitting across the table from him. He needed to get him as far away from the village as possible before Daniels arrived. It would take a bit of ass-kissing on his part, even if it meant eating the soup.

His stomach protested again.

"I was informed a Ms. Newman would be accompanying Mr. Daniels," Dr. Sanchez continued.

Harold held his breath and ladled soup into his mouth.

"She could not make it?" The researcher made it a question.

Damn it! The man had been informed of the stupid broad's decision to follow Daniels into the wilds. What else was this man aware of?

The soup slid down his throat into his empty stomach. He held his breath and took another spoonful to play for time.

"No. I'm afraid some complications arose and she was...uh...detained, as well."

"That is too bad. I was looking forward to

meeting her again. Oh, well. Another time, perhaps."

Bennett made a stab at eating more of the strong smelling liquid in front of him. After the first two spoonfuls, he started to gag. The coarse texture filled his mouth and he cursed as he forced it down. Grabbing his napkin as if it were a life line he turned his head away from the researcher and pressed the cloth to his lips. God, how could they live on this putrid slime?

If Jake Daniels was here right now he'd kill him on the spot for putting him through this living hell. Why couldn't he have just signed those damn contracts at the meeting the other day and be done with it? Why was he rechecking the route this late in the negotiations? Thomas was right. Holmes must be on to them.

Thankfully, Sanchez seemed unaware of his distress over the soup.

It took Harold a minute to realize Sanchez was still speaking about meeting up with the damn broad.

"Yes, of course, another time," Bennett mumbled. His stomach rumbled.

Like in five to ten when she was released from prison for money laundering. By the time they had it all figured out, he and Grapley would be long gone.

Harold held his snicker in check. What a perfect set up. Best of all, Miss Newman wasn't even aware of her fate. She'd championed his side at the meeting so eloquently. But, he didn't have time to dwell on his good luck; he had to get Sanchez moving. He doubted Daniels had given up and turned back.

Harold ate as much of the soup as he could keep down before pushing the bowl to the center of the table.

"Sorry, the stomach's a bit off today."

"No matter. Drink some of our *Palom de leche.* It will make your stomach feel much better as well as

83

Carol Henry

fill you up a bit."

He didn't want any more of their putrid shit. These natives were going to poison him before he could get out of their jungle. God, he couldn't wait to get back to civilization.

"I'm anxious to recheck the pipeline route as arranged. I understand a portion of the logged area has been turned into a farming operation. That's good. That's good."

"As planned, I will take you there. Perhaps we should wait until after the rains come this afternoon. It will be better tomorrow."

Harold froze. He didn't have time to wait out another torrential storm for God's sake. It was the rainy season. He'd be waiting forever.

"I'd prefer to go now. It shouldn't take long. I planned to head back early in the morning. Don't want to hold up contracts any longer than necessary, you understand."

Sanchez hesitated. Was the man going to refuse? Bennett took a deep breath when the researcher finally stood up, a smile on his face.

"Of course. You will be surprised at what we have done with what we have learned in regards to intercropping. The program with the university has been much help. Students recently visited to learn and study the problems we face."

"Intercropping? Oh. Yes. Growing two crops side-by-side. What crops are you working on?" *Like he really cared.*

"We are growing cabbage with our bananas in one area. And a major staple here, manioc, and of course nuts. It seems to be going very well so far. Using this area for the pipeline will help save unharvested land further along, don't you agree?"

"Naturally. We should get started, then. I'm anxious to see the route along this area," Bennett stated. He stood and followed Sanchez, hoping he sounded convincingly interested.

"We must walk. It is still muddy from yesterday's rain and too much mud for vehicles to get through, you understand. It is the rainy season, after all."

No shit!

Sanchez kept up his monologue as they made their way through the village toward the road that led to the fields. Harold kept up the pretense of listening, his mind on how he was going to keep the man away from the village for several hours. He hadn't thought that far ahead, and he was beginning to have doubts he could pull it off. He would just have to keep egging the man on so they would go deeper and deeper into the jungle. He'd think of something along the way.

"There will be no cabbage at this time as you may be aware. But then you are not interested so very much in this aspect of our research here. You are more anxious to follow the trail of the new pipeline that will bring fuel to our big cities, no?"

Bennett shook his head in the affirmative. He was definitely more anxious, to get Sanchez away from the village before Daniels showed up. If he could detain the researcher long enough so that Daniels would move on, he'd tie the man to a tree overnight if that's what it took. If Sanchez didn't show when Daniels arrived, Daniels would have no option but to call it a day and turn around and go back to Manaus in time to sign the contracts Friday morning. Harold couldn't control the pleasure that washed over him. Things that happened in the jungle stayed in the jungle. He smiled as he walked behind Dr. Sanchez. A researcher who went about 'searching' for things for long periods of time wouldn't be missed right away.

Bennett pulled his soiled handkerchief from his pocket and wiped at the sweat on his forehead and around the back of his neck. He wadded it up and tucked it back in his pocket. His best guesstimate was that Daniels was behind him by at least five to six hours. His own guides had provided a shorter route crossing through the restricted *Vale do Javari*. Tracker had assured him that he had communicated with the indigenous people in that area. They agreed to let Bennett's group pass without incident in exchange for a large delivery of food. True to their word, they hadn't seen a single *Kulina* or *Korubo* the entire time. Using flat boats once they hit the *Juti* River, they had left the smelly four-footed jackasses behind. Tracker had confirmed that they had successfully circled around Daniels without them even knowing it.

Harold continued walking, deep in thought, ignoring the researcher's constant yapping. The man reminded him of his wife back home. He rubbed at his throbbing temples, took a deep breath through his nose and let it out slowly. It didn't help. The sinus pressure tightened.

Suddenly something Sanchez said caught his attention.

"I'm sorry this is taking so long. We could have used the mules that I sent to assist in your travels. Somehow you did not connect?"

"Yes. I mean, no. We didn't connect." A sharp pain flashed behind his eyeballs. "The guides assigned to me must have misunderstood. You know how it is with so many dialects. Such confusion."

"No matter. It will take us a little longer to reach the perimeter of the field and the route. There is a road now, thanks to the loggers. Although muddy, it is easier access to our farming and the pipeline route. As I said, I am afraid your shoes will suffer."

Bennett cringed as he looked down at his soiled shoes again. Scuffed, caked with mud, and wet clear

Amazon Connection

through to his socks, the shine was long gone. At this point, it was worth it.

"No matter," he said, keeping it short. His breathing labored, his stomach rolled. Bile rose in his throat. He swallowed it back down and kept walking. Sanchez droned on and on. He didn't give a damn about the farming methods they'd instituted with their intercropping. He didn't care that they replanted hardwood trees to rebalance nature and the world at large. He could give a shit what these people did. As long as their government signed those contracts so Thomas could process the funds and funnel the money to their Swiss bank accounts.

Sweat trickled down his forehead.

His stomach lurched again.

They kept walking.

Forty-five minutes later, Bennett's stomach retched. He made a bee-line for the side of the rutted roadway. Hands on knees, he bent forward and emptied his stomach of what little squash soup he'd consumed. He rummaged in his pockets and pulled out the soiled handkerchief. It was better than nothing. He swiped the stiff cloth over his mouth and chin and threw it on the ground. He returned to the roadway on wobbly legs.

"Sorry about that," he rasped, then cleared his throat. "It's the heat. How much further before we reach the main section of the route?"

"Maybe two more miles, then the route goes into the forest. We'll be out of this heat soon. Perhaps you would like to rest a moment before we continue. There are bananas just over there. The potassium will be of help, no? I will get you one if you like."

No he didn't like. The last thing he wanted now was a heavy banana churning around in his stomach. "Thanks. I'll be fine."

Sanchez reached in his backpack, pulled out a small bottle of water and handed it to him.

87

Carol Henry

"It is warm, I apologize. But it will help, no?"

"Yes. Thank you." If he wasn't so thirsty, he'd throw the bottle in the man's face. He'd had it. He didn't want to see the pipeline. He knew where it was. He didn't care about the farming operation. And he certainly didn't give a damn about the indigenous people, their endangered species, or the potential medical cures Holly Newman had gone on and on about over the last couple of months. And right now he could care less about Sanchez. There wasn't a single drop of sweat on the man's face.

He was tired of being polite.

Hell, he was just plain tired.

He should have sent Grapley into the Rainforest. His brother-in-law did nothing but sit on his lazy ass in front of the computer. He deserved a lesser cut of the take for doing nothing but running his fingers over the keyboard hacking into bank accounts. How hard could it be to punch numbers on a keyboard all damn day? The more he thought about it, the more he wondered if he could trust Thomas. He only had Thomas' word that he'd get his fair share.

"You do not look well," Sanchez said. "Perhaps we should go back?"

"No! Keep moving," Bennett snapped. He rubbed his right hand down over his stomach and around the back side of his ribs. And his concealed snub-nosed .38. His hand itched to pull it from its hiding place. He didn't care if Sanchez was on to him or not. He was tired of playing this stupid game.

Bennett's head pounded. His legs shook, his head buzzed, and he didn't want to listen to another word about intercropping and cabbages. He pulled the gun from his holster and pointed it at Sanchez's back.

A pain shot through his chest. He clutched his heart with his left hand, and tried to steady himself as his knees dipped. He ignored the pain and smiled as he rubbed the smooth, warm, metal of the gun he held tight in his right hand.

He smiled.

Sanchez kept walking.

Bennett bent his finger on the trigger and pulled the hammer back. He'd get the researcher's attention, all right.

Sanchez kept moving. The man kept talking as if he didn't know he'd just had a gun pulled on him.

"Stop!" Bennett yelled, planting his feet wide to steady his stance, the hammering pain in his chest relentless. "Take one more step and you're dead. I'm sick to death of this god-forsaken cesspool of a jungle. I'm this close to pulling this here trigger."

Sanchez stopped.

Bennett raised his eyebrows and leveled the gun. The bastard was finally taking notice.

Sanchez turned to face him.

The cocky bastard didn't stand a chance.

He saw the dare in the researcher's eyes, the pinched smile on his tanned face, and the taut defiant body.

Bennett's vision blurred. He blinked hard, but kept his stance steady. But the gasp coming from deep within when he spotted the other man's gun was anything but controlled. Sanchez aimed a small pistol straight at his chest.

Chapter Nine

Holly sat on a semi-dry mound of earth next to the overflowing muddy waters of the *Juti* River. She slapped at a sudden pin prick on the back of her neck. Instead of finding a thin, poisoned dart sticking out of her body as feared, her trembling hand came away smeared with a large dead mosquito and a spot of her own blood.

It wasn't much, but still reminded her of the dead animals in the blood encased sacks. She forced herself to stop thinking about the dead monkeys and reached in her pocket for the small spray can of DEET. Damn, it was almost gone. She squirted it above her head anyway. A fine mist floated over her hair, neck and shoulders.

"Take it easy with that stuff," Jake cautioned.

"I just got bit by a dinosaur-sized mosquito. If I don't use something the insects will suck me dry."

"Did you take Mefloquine tablets before you left New York?"

"Of course." She wasn't that green behind the ears, as her grandfather used to say.

"Good. You can't be too careful."

The tablets the travel nurse had given her had made her nauseous the first few days but she'd been told that it was nothing compared to actually contracting malaria. She'd stopped complaining and made sure the rest of her shots were up to date, as well.

Exhausted, Holly settled back to rest her aching muscles, not to mention her blistered feet. She knew better than to take her shoes off again, no matter how tempting.

"Once we board the boat we should reach the village in a couple of hours," Jake informed her. "From the look of that sky, I'd say we're in for a downpour. If we don't get underway soon, I'm afraid we'll be caught in the deluge."

Right now a refreshing shower in any form would be welcomed. And she wanted answers.

What were they really doing out here? And what made Jake think Harold or Thomas had anything to do with their misfortunes?

"Enough small talk, Jake. I still want to know what's going on. So far you've insinuated that Harold Bennett and Thomas Grapley turned in false maps. Why would they do that? And what has any of that got to do with them being responsible for our misfortunes so far? I went over their routes several times. They made the changes I suggested. I approved the final version. I didn't see anything wrong with them."

Holly watched his poker face fall back into place. She hated when he did that.

"Because that's exactly what they want you to believe," he finally answered, not quite meeting her eyes. "That their route doesn't infringe on the indigenous people."

"I don't follow." She didn't understand his hesitation.

"It's a shorter route." He stated, this time looking right into her eyes. "Your map shows the route skirting around the *Vale Do Javari*, when in fact the actual route they've laid out goes right through it. That's why we came so close to entering it when Ivan stopped us."

"And you knew this how?" He was beginning to make sense. Sort of.

"Why else would we have ended up there?"

Carol Henry

He was watching her as if she had all the answers. She didn't. She knew the area was off-limits. She never would have approved such a route otherwise. But what she still didn't understand was why the two men would do such a thing.

"Derrick put Bennett and Grapley on the project after their last botched assignment hoping they were honest mistakes. I was busy with another assignment in Alaska at the time, and he didn't fill me in on the details. Derrick refused to promote them for the second time, and of course the two men weren't happy about it. Their indiscretions weren't exactly criminal. Their jobs turned out satisfactorily in the end. So, when Mr. Delgado contacted Derrick about a few discrepancies with the project, Derrick sent me down to get enough evidence against them to justify firing them."

"How do they benefit from falsifying the route, unless it's to discredit GlennCorp?"

Again Jake hesitated as if trying to decide what to tell her. Holly waited, then relaxed as he filled her in.

"Derrick thinks they plan to skim from the project by giving the Brazilians a longer route which will cost more to build. In turn, they've given GlennCorp a shorter version. The Brazilian payout will be more than what GlennCorp expects. As soon as we sign those contracts and the money changes hands, they plan to set their scheme in motion and walk off with a bundle. Once they disappear, probably to Colombia, there's no way to catch up with them. We can't let that happen."

Holly jumped to her feet, glaring at Jake. "I knew it! I knew you were holding something back. Why didn't you tell me this before? Why the big secret?"

"It had to look as if nothing was wrong—everything needed to remain status quo. We didn't want to spook Bennett and Grapley into fleeing and getting away with it. We still can't. We need to catch them with their hands in the cookie jar."

"No wonder you were pumping me for information about them." Holly turned and sat back down with a sigh. She looked up river for a moment before turning back to Jake. "So, do you think Dr. Sanchez is in on it with them?"

"Not sure, but I need to catch those two in the act first, then find out who the insider is that's helping them."

****

Jake shifted from foot to foot. Had he told her too much? She had a way of getting him to talk when he was the one who was supposed to get her to do the talking. The urge to take her in his arms and apologize held him in check. How could he apologize, when he wasn't telling her everything?

Damn it, every time he decided she wasn't involved, she started sticking up for the two cretins. She might not know who the real insider was, but letting her think it was Sanchez either played into her hand, or didn't amount to a bag of beans.

He cleared his throat.

"I'm used to working alone, Holly, not sharing this kind of information unless it's necessary."

"I appreciate you sharing it with me, now. Thanks, Jake." Holly smiled.

Damn, the woman was getting to him. Her smile looked like the real deal.

You're an ass, Daniels. A royal jack-ass!

He ran his fingers through his hair and stepped back, wanting to wring Bennett and Grapley's fat necks. The hell with being fired. The men were scum, and the sooner they were put behind bars the better.

"So, let's work on this together, shall we? Tell me what you know."

He watched her face fall, her eyes shuttered. She looked guilty as hell.

Ah, crap!

"I told you everything I know." She turned from him and looked out over the river. "Their work ethics were without question."

She kept her back to him. He liked the view.

He shook his head to marshal his thoughts back to the matter at hand.

"Getting close to the *Vale Do Javari* is pretty conclusive evidence that they're trying to swindle both the Brazilian government and GlennCorp. After we meet with Dr. Sanchez, we can head back to Manaus and work out the appropriate route."

Holly stepped farther away from him, taking her exotic intoxicating scent with her.

"You weren't kidding were you?" Holly surprised him by turning back and asking.

The soulful, hurt look in her eyes wedged deep in his heart. "Do you really think those two are responsible for everything that's happened to us out here?"

She sounded resolved, defeated. Was she starting to believe him? Or was she playing him? Trying to figure out if he suspected her? Was she really worried that either Bennett or Grapley, or one of their goons was following them and didn't know it? That would account for her reaction to everything that'd happened to them so far. But, he didn't know her well enough to determine whether or not she was putting on an act. He needed more proof that she wasn't involved.

"If they're the ones who stole our mules, they're ahead of us and on their way to meet up with Dr. Sanchez," Jake said. "How far ahead depends on when they confiscated the mules during the night, what route they took to reach this river, and what kind of transportation they have now."

Amazon Connection

"Why would they want to get to the village ahead of us? It doesn't make sense." Holly leaned back against the tree trunk. He didn't have the heart to tell her there was a green snake coiled in the curve of a branch high above her, its head dangling over hers. He kept an eye on it, hoping their boat would come soon.

"I'm not sure what they're up to," he said in a lowered voice, not wanting to incite the reptile. Guilty or not, he didn't want to see her bitten by a deadly, viper. "But we're going to find out. I think I see the guides coming with our boats. Why don't you come over here so we'll be ready to board when they pull in?"

He hoped the distraction worked, and that the snake wasn't interested. Holly stood and walked to the water's edge. Jake smiled, relieved.

Whew! At least he'd saved her from one potential catastrophe.

Five minutes later, settled in long, flat boats equipped with small outboard motors, they were motoring up the river toward the village. Holly sat in the front of the boat, leaving Jake to take the seat in the back, as they'd done before.

The river narrowed, curved, then widened as the three boats meandered along the riverbanks teeming with tropical vegetation. The guides searching for the mules had not returned. Holly wondered just how long they'd continue to look for them. She didn't like the idea of the poor animals wandering around lost in the rainforest. She knew what that felt like.

Spider monkeys screeched overhead, swinging from branch to branch. River otters slithered comically in the mud along the banks and plunged into the water to look for a meal. Colorful macaws noisily made their presence known as a few flew overhead in the noontime sun.

A huge cloud mass was blowing in from the

North, breaking up the sunshine and blue sky, but looked to be a long way off. Holly's anxiety seeped away under the spell of the exotic splendors of nature that surrounded them. For the first time since coming to Brazil she found herself able to truly enjoy the rainforest.

Most of her time had been spent trying to keep dry during the Amazon's rainy season. Her forays hadn't taken her this deep into the interior and she was beginning to wonder just how effective her reports were. She was beginning to think Jake was right to question her. What did she really know about any of this? She'd been trying to put a brave front on everything her whole life. Meeting up with real challenges out here in the rainforest made her face the truth. She wasn't just a wimp. She was a phony.

No more. She'd help Jake nail those two bums no matter what it took. Including dealing with the great outdoors. If Harold or Thomas were following them, she'd help Jake figure it out. She'd be more alert.

More brave.

Not such a wimp!

Thanks to the poinsettia paste the blisters hadn't bothered her in the last couple of hours. Even the drone of the outboard motor didn't detract from the new frame of mind she'd decided to adopt. Jake had finally shared the facts of his case with her. That meant he trusted her. A warm and fuzzy heat filled her. A wide smile spread across her face. Mr. Sinfully Handsome wasn't so bad after all.

"Look. Look." Ivan startled her as they rounded yet another awe-inspiring bend in the river. He pointed to a pocked cliff amass with vivid color— scarlet, gold, hyacinth, and emerald macaws were perched together by the hundreds on the face of the rocks.

Holly gazed in awe at the incredible colors and the hundreds of birds hugging the cliff. *Aaah, Macaws. True love birds.* They mated for life, sometimes spending close to fifty years with the same partner. They were jealous creatures, guarding their partners carefully. What a romantic thought. Humans could certainly take a few lessons from these beautiful birds.

Tony hadn't fit the bill, but someone like Jake Daniels had integrity. Alright, so with his good looks and positive, take-control attitude, he probably had women drooling over him all the time. If he ever decided to settle down, she couldn't picture him being unfaithful.

Jake hadn't so much as used her attraction to him against her. He hadn't used it to get information or to coerce her into having a one-night stand. And he had to be aware of that attraction between them. On the one hand she was offended that he hadn't taken advantage of her when he'd had the chance, but on the other, she respected him for it.

Jake definitely wasn't a Tony.

Holly watched the macaws for long moments, the stunning sight breathtaking. Magical. Her eyes misted, the cliff-side became a blur of psychedelic color. Despite being surrounded by her guides and Jake, her heart beat hollow. Oh, to be so cared for to the point that someone would fight for her, protect her, and want to spend the rest of their life with her.

Maudlin wasn't her style. It had to be this amazingly romantic Amazonian rainforest that was turning her insides to mush.

She didn't want mush.

She didn't want lonely.

When had life become so complicated?

****

Jake caught the glistening brightness in Holly's eyes seconds before she turned her back on him again. If it wasn't for risking tipping the boat over, and everyone ending up as piranha bait, he'd act on the urge to take her in his arms. And never let her go.

He shouldn't care about her as much as he did, but damn, he couldn't help himself. She was more than a beautiful woman. She was strong, and she met danger head on.

Falling for someone this fast was not a good sign.

Nothing can come of it.

Stay focused. Get the job done. Get in, get out.

Holly's sexy feathered earring dangled against her neck; it drove him crazy. Her sun-kissed skin begged to be caressed.

He swallowed. Hard.

One more day in this jungle keeping his distance from Holly Newman was going to drive him crazy. He admired her tenacity to deal with her fears, get control and move on. She kept on going even when he knew she was worn out and her feet were killing her. She'd kept her cool when the anaconda swam ahead of them upriver before slithering down a side channel. She'd remained composed when the large bird-eating tarantula crawled out of its hole under the dead leaves and scooted over her foot. Okay, so she'd up and fainted on him when the natives rushed from the hedge thinking they were attacking instead of saving them, but once she realized they were safe, she'd recovered splendidly. Even her blistered feet and the sight of so much blood hadn't slowed her down. Not many women he knew would have the nerve to follow him into the jungle afraid of anything that could possibly jump out at them. Not to mention be able to hold up under the types of pressures they'd had to face so far. They had been abandoned, gotten lost. After the initial shock, she faced it and hadn't become a blathering, demanding, sobbing, nagging woman.

And that was saying a lot.

Jake smiled. Holly Newman was one hell-of-a lady. He hoped like hell she wasn't involved in laundering money from GlennCorp. He'd hate to have her arrested along with Bennett and Grapley.

They rounded two more bends in the river shrouded in heavy foliage. The sagging, dark clouds moved in, and the rains began. Slowly at first, a fine drizzle, then a thick mist. Holly dug out her hooded rain jacket and slipped into it minutes before the rain came down in earnest. Steam rose from the river making visibility difficult.

The boat came to a sudden, grinding stop. Jake sat helpless as Holly was thrown forward. Luckily she grabbed onto the side of the boat.

"A sandbar," Ivan called over the spill of the rain.

The sandbar was overgrown with brush.

Shit! He hoped like hell there were no alligators hiding in that brush.

Chapter Ten

Holly's foot caught under the seat, saving her from going overboard. She landed on her butt in the bottom of the boat and got totally soaked. Sitting on the wooden bench-type seat didn't help either.

Rain filled the boat as if it was pouring straight out of a faucet.

The afternoon rain continued to pelt down on them with a vengeance. With the rain came more steamy humidity. Her clear, vinyl, hooded rain jacket clung annoyingly, making it difficult to move.

For the umpteenth time she berated herself for losing her temper and insisting she follow Jake into the jungle. She knew she'd said it often enough, but, really, what had she been thinking? If there was any consolation right now, it was that everyone else was just as drenched. No sense in complaining—no one would listen or sympathize with her anyway.

The rain thundered making talk impossible. Huge raindrops splattered in the river and splashed back up into the boat.

Holly looked behind her and barely made out the silhouettes of the guides bent over scooping out buckets full of water. It was no use. Rain was coming down faster than they were able to scoop it out. How long they had been at it, she didn't know. She only knew she wished she was some place else, anywhere, but here.

"How're you doing?" Jake asked, stepping over the center of the boat, looming over her with a big grin on his face. "Wild, isn't it? When it rains, it pours, huh?"

She couldn't answer. His smile mesmerized her. He reminded her of her ten-year-old nephew playing in the rain. The man was actually enjoying himself. His hair lay plastered against his forehead, and hugged his neck. Unlike her nephew, Jake's shirt clung provocatively to his wet skin as water ran in tantalizing rivulets over his firm, bulging biceps. He did nothing to protect himself from the deluge.

He could be Tarzan himself standing next to her. The man was in his element. She couldn't take her eyes off him. Denying the feelings that had been coursing through her veins since they'd met was useless. His smile was her undoing.

Shrouded in mist, the rain continued to sluice over their bodies, while water continued to rise. And all she could think about was what it would be like to be kissed by Jake Daniels—a real bone-shattering kiss.

She couldn't breathe.

Holly's heartbeat thundered wildly. She'd said she was going to follow him into the jungle come rain or come shine, but she hadn't meant it quite so literally. Her smile broadened automatically. They were in this adventure together. And what an adventure it was turning out to be.

His grin widened. His eyes sparkled with speculation. Had he read her mind?

The boat lurched sideways. Jake grabbed her arm to keep her from falling overboard.

"We aren't far from shore," he shouted over the pelting rain. "Ivan says it's not that deep here. We can get out and wade in. We're up to our knees and soaked already anyway."

"What? You want me to get in that river? Are you mad?" Holly shouted back.

"I'm sorry." Jake cupped his ear. "I can't hear you," he mouthed. "Let me help you over."

"There better not be any alligators lurking close by, Daniels."

He jumped over the side of the sinking boat before she could stop him. The boat tipped. Holly couldn't tell if the water was flowing out of the boat or back in.

Jake held his hands out to her. She could only stare at him, and at the other guides who were now parading through the muddy river on their way to shore. Unless she planned to stay in the middle of the sandbar all by herself, she knew she had to take her chances and trudged through the mud with the rest of them.

She leaned over and placed her hands on Jake's shoulders only to have him grab her and swing her over his shoulder.

"Put me down," Holly sputtered. "I can walk on my own." Being thrown over his shoulder like a sack of feed was anything but romantic. She pounded her fists on his back.

He ignored her.

"If you don't put me down right this second, Jake Daniels, I'm going to scream my fool head off."

"It won't do you any good," he yelled over his shoulder. "In case you haven't noticed, it's raining too hard for anyone to hear. They know I have you so I doubt they'll think you're in trouble. Besides, everyone's gone on ahead."

"How can I notice? All I can see is your backside."

Which brought her up short. It was a nice firm, rain-slicked back side.

She didn't like the sound of his chuckle as he proceeded to carry her the short distance across the riverbed and up the slippery, muddy embankment to the shelter of the rainforest's dense canopy. Under the protection of the trees the rain was a heavy drizzle compared to the torrential downpour out in the open. Regardless, the heat from Jake's body penetrated her wet clothes. The friction of their bodies rubbing against each other sparked something inside her that was hard to deny. Her attraction to Jake Daniels was getting harder to ignore.

Think...? Who the hell am I suppose to think about?

Who cares?

Holly welcomed Jake's body heat, a sweet torture as he slid her slowly and snugly down his firm, sexy body, letting her know in no uncertain terms what her closeness was doing to him, too. The friction seeped through every scrap of clothing she wore. It penetrated deep into each and every excited pore and coursed through every single vein like molten volcanic flow. Her body sizzled with it. Her feet touched the damp, soggy earth, grounding the electrical current flowing between them.

Her legs buckled.

Jake caught her and pulled her to him before she crumbled to a heap at his feet. She saw the hunger in his eyes and couldn't move even if they had been standing in sub-zero temperatures. He lowered his head, his eyes never leaving hers. He drew her up off the rainforest floor and closed his eyes as their lips touched.

Ivan shouted to them to catch up. The spell was broken.

Jake released her.

Confused, Holly blurted out the first thing she could think of.

"How much farther is the village?"

He smiled, knowingly. She felt heat rise up her neck and prick her cheeks.

"Not far, I hope," his voice unsteady. "Do your feet hurt? Can you walk?"

Other than burning from his closeness, she

103

didn't feel a thing.

"I can walk."

"That's my girl. We need to catch up with the others before they get out of sight. I'll put more salve on your feet when we get there."

Thinking about Jake smoothing salve on her feet was too erotic to contemplate. Her insides tingled at the thought. She trembled and closed her eyes as if that would make the feelings disappear. It didn't. Instead, they intensified.

Jake took her hand. "Let's get a move on. We don't want to be stranded again." He dragged her deeper into the rainforest.

They caught up with the others and followed along single file in the drizzling rain. Before long they wound their way back toward the shoreline. The rain had let up some and another mile up they came to the village.

Mist shrouded the encampment. It looked still and sinister.

"Where is everyone?" Holly whispered.

"The rain must have driven them inside."

Ivan pointed to the left. A pavilion dominated one end of the small village. Holly nodded.

"It'll be good to be dry again," she said.

What an understatement. *So much for needing a shower.* They were all soaked.

A row of shacks, barely visible through the mist, hugged the perimeter of the rainforest on the opposite side of the clearing. Holly saw other houses built up on stilts hanging over the water's edge. She stepped under the protection of the large open-air pavilion. The floor was damp from rain spatter, but thankfully, the center area was dry.

Several of the guides made their way across the encampment to the houses across the way.

"Sit, please. I go find Doctor Sanchez," Ivan instructed.

Holly shrugged out of her dripping raincoat and welcomed the fresh air against her damp, hot skin. She pulled the scrunchy from her hair and raked her fingers through the long, tangled strands then pulled her hair back into a neater ponytail to keep it off her neck and shoulders. She was more than happy to sit down.

A petite girl with dark eyes and auburn hair came from behind a screened-in area at the far end of the building, a frown on her face. Perhaps they were intruding and the girl was upset with their presence. Brightly beaded necklaces of seeds and feathers circled her neck and jangled as she walked. A myriad of colorful, tightly woven bracelets lined her arms like Ivan's, clear up to her elbow. Holly smiled and was surprised to see the girl smile back at her.

"The Doctor. He gone," the young girl finally spoke in broken English. "He not come back."

Ivan and the girl broke into Portuguese while a handful of the returning guides stood by listening.

"What's wrong?" Holly stood and leaned toward Jake. "They sound frantic. Has something happened to Dr. Sanchez?"

"I don't know. They're talking too fast for me to follow what's being said. We'll have to wait and ask Ivan."

"I have a bad feeling about this, Jake. A real bad feeling." Holly clung to Jake's arm. He slipped his arm around her waist and pulled her close.

Her thoughts ran wild, each scenario worse than the first. She couldn't help thinking about her nightmare last night. Had it been an omen of things to come instead of things that had already happened?

A shiver raced down her spine.

Dreams. They were impossible to decipher.

"Don't fall apart on me now, Sweetheart," Jake

whispered in her ear. "We're safe. Any number of things could have happened to him. I suspect he's merely seeking shelter somewhere waiting for the rain and mist to let up so he can find his way back."

"I hope you're right." Holly's spirits drooped along with the rest of her. "How can they stand this dampness day after day?"

"Once the sun comes back out you'll be wishing for a cool shower again. The humidity will kick in as the sun soaks up the moisture from the ground. It'll be hot." Jake squeezed her shoulders before letting go. He pushed her in the direction of one of the long benches. "Sit and get off your feet. I'll see what's going on then we'll find someplace to go and get out of these damp clothes."

The conversation with the young girl, Pilar, and Ivan finally ended. Pilar pointed toward the other side of the village. Ivan approached Jake, nose flared, teeth clenched.

"White man come. The Doctor, he take him to field to see crops. They gone long time. Villagers worried."

"Is someone searching for him?" Jake asked.

"Miguel. He not come back. Others, they wait for rain to stop. They go now."

"How long has he been missing?" Jake asked, checking his watch as if that would tell him what he wanted to know.

"Long time. Maybe half day." Ivan pointed to one of the wood-framed cabins across the compound. "You sleep there."

Jake nodded his thanks. The cabin had a solid looking door and screens on the window openings. A kerosene lantern hung from a hook outside the door. The cabin reminded him of a hundred other cabins he'd slept in at the various scout camps he'd attended over the years. At least there'd be more room in the cabin then there had been in the two-man pup-tent last night.

"Let's get out of these wet clothes," Jake said. "There isn't much else we can do here except wait."

He picked up his backpack, slung it over his shoulder and headed toward the cabin Ivan had indicated. Holly followed.

Jake opened the door to the cabin and entered the shaded room. He dropped his gear on the floor with a sigh of relief. Holly followed suit.

"I hope you have a dry pair of shoes in there somewhere," Jake stated. "I suggest you give those blisters a chance to dry off before we put anything on them."

A simple wooden straight-back chair sat in the corner. Holly sat down, untied her shoes, and kicked them off in turn.

"Ahhhh, I've been dying to do that all day."

"As soon as I change, I'll rub more salve on your feet."

"You change first. I'll wait outside." Holly limped toward the front steps and sat down, leaving the door open.

"Get your butt back in here, Holly. You can turn your back and I'll do the same if it'll make you feel more comfortable." Jake reached down, grabbed her hand and yanked her back into the coolness of the cabin.

Right into his arms. She was plastered against him. He looked into her eyes, then proceeded to trail tiny kisses along her cheek, her chin, her neck. He felt her stiffen as his wandering lips found their way back up to hers. And he was lost. She relaxed, then clung to him giving kiss for kiss, both of them unwilling to pull apart.

Finally, coming up for air, Jake nestled her head in his shoulder, holding her tight.

"I've wanted to do this all day," he whispered. "You've been driving me crazy. You and that damn earring."

"Jake, I don't think this is such a smart idea." Her voice was shaky.

He leaned back and looked into her aroused eyes and watched as she wrestled with her emotions. There was no denying her reaction to him. He covered her quivering lips with his once more.

Her arms slid around his neck as she kissed him back. He came undone. He felt alive for the first time in his life.

He deepened the kiss.

The world exploded.

The door flew open.

Ivan rushed in and doused the fire that was burning out of control between them.

"Come. Come. The Doctor. He is hurt," Ivan's distressed pleas penetrated their heated embrace.

"What happened?" Jake's passion-induced mind slowly cleared. Still in the throes of that world shattering kiss, it took a minute to comprehend what Ivan was saying. Unable to break the connection from Holly entirely, he held on to her a moment longer. When her breathing steadied, he shifted into alert status.

"What happened?" he repeated.

"He is shot. Come. You see."

Jake followed Ivan out the door. "I'll be right back," he called over his shoulder to Holly. "You stay and get changed. I'll find out what's going on."

"No way are you leaving me behind." Holly followed them to the door where she quickly bent down to retrieve her shoes. "I'm coming with you."

Too late, Holly was talking to herself. She stood looking through an empty doorway as Jake and Ivan ran across the compound to the pavilion.

Not to be outdone, Holly said the heck with dry clothes and took off after Jake.

Barefoot.

Amazon Connection

The shock of the soft, thick mud squishing between her toes startled her. She stopped mid-step, the childishness of it turned to wild and carefree abandon. Then the urgency in Ivan's voice prevailed and she rushed to the pavilion.

When she reached the pavilion she found Dr. Sanchez lying on the floor covered in blood. She quickly turned around and covered her mouth. All thoughts of the kiss she and Jake had shared moments ago were wiped from her mind. She shut her eyes to try to erase the sight of the wounded man lying at her feet. And the oozing blood.

The image persisted. She opened her eyes again and sat at one of the tables.

She could do this. She'd promised herself she could do this.

She wouldn't pass out from the sight of blood. Not this time.

"He's been shot," Jake confirmed Ivan's report.

A tall Brazilian stood next to Ivan, his reddish brown hair curled tightly against his head, his blue eyes large and concerned as he looked down at the prone man on the floor. "He lost much blood," the tall man stated.

Holly's head began to sway. She forced herself to take several deep breaths, then laid her head in folded hands on the table. The stench from the soggy compound, now basking in the late afternoon heat, mingled with the scent of fresh iron-rich blood penetrated the air. The cloying combination made breathing difficult. She wanted to vomit.

Jake knelt beside Dr. Sanchez and felt for the man's pulse.

"He's alive," he reaffirmed.

A loud, collective sigh filled the pavilion. Holly looked up, relieved, and put her head back down.

"He needs a doctor." Jake turned to Miguel. "What happened?"

109

Carol Henry

After a short conversation between Miguel and Ivan, Ivan reported back to Jake.

"Miguel say the doctor go to field with short dark-hair man in suit. They go to see pipeline trail. Miguel go look for them when they not come back. He find doctor on ground."

Oh my God. It sounded like Harold Bennett.

Jake was right. Harold Bennett had followed them. He was the one who arranged to have them stranded. And, he stole the mules!

Why?

What the hell was really going on here?

Holly was going to be sick and it had nothing to do with the blood pooling around Dr. Sanchez' body.

"We need to get him to a hospital." She heard Jake say. "Is there someone in the village who can help him in the meantime? A medicine man perhaps?"

"Medicine man long way that way." Miguel pointed in the opposite direction.

"We need to stop the bleeding and find a way to get medical help."

Jake tore at the man's shirt to check the wound. Blood oozed over the side of the man's body.

Holly blanched.

Jake applied pressure to the wound with the palm of his hand to help stop the flow.

Holly watched in amazement at how adept Jake was at handling the situation.

"How far is the nearest town? What is the fastest way to get there?" Jake called out.

Holly heard the concern in Jake's voice. She looked around and was astonished to see everyone standing around in a trance-like state. Jake needed help.

Without thinking, Holly darted forward. She stepped over the bleeding body and knelt next to it, all the while focusing on Jake instead of the man

110

lying on the floor. She closed her eyes, opened them, and looked down at Dr. Sanchez.

"Is the bullet still inside?" Tentatively she touched the body and was startled to find it cool to the touch. "How could anyone be so cold on such a hot day?" she asked in a hushed tone, as if the wounded man might hear her.

"He's lost a lot of blood. Help me turn him over so we can see if there's an exit wound."

Holly took deep, steadying breaths as she gently pushed while Jake tugged at the man's right side. She marveled at the way Jake maintained as much pressure on the chest wound as possible and still managed to take off his shirt. He folded it and placed it over the chest wound for a compress. He raised his knee and pressed it against the make-shift bandage to hold it in place, then leaned over to check the man's back.

"Did it go through his heart?" Holly asked.

"He'd be dead by now if it did," Jake said. "Apparently whoever shot him had poor aim. I don't dare let up pressure on his chest. Can you see a wound on his back?"

"Yes. Oh my God, Jake. It's awful." Holly shut her eyes and shook her head trying to dispel the sight of the angry-looking wound covered in blood. She couldn't pass out now. Jake needed her.

"Hang in there, Holly."

Pilar appeared with a clean towel. Holly automatically took it and applied it to the open wound on the man's back.

"Jake..."

"Holly, the man is dying. He's our only hope of finding out what's going on, or who shot him. We've got to get this bleeding stopped."

Holly shut her eyes and willed herself to show these people she was no wimp. She looked up to see the young girl, Pilar. Ivan stood next to her, concern written all over his face. She couldn't let them down.

She wouldn't let them down.

She wouldn't let Jake down.

Holly pressed the cloth tight against the man's back. Ivan handed Jake a long, towel-like piece of material. Jake wrapped it around Dr. Sanchez' chest. Once the make-shift bandage was secure, she helped Jake gently roll the man onto his back.

And saw her blood-covered hands.

Oh, God! Oh, God! Oh, God!

Holly shook her hands. The blood had already dried into her pores, the heavy smell of iron surrounded her. She jumped from the circle of men and ran back to the cabin, her arms and hands flailing. The blood on her hands tightened. She held her breath, her head light. She splashed through a puddle and slid to a stop. Bending down she splayed her hands into the muddy water and scrubbed the blood from her hands. She looked back at the scene she'd just left. Thankfully no one was paying any attention to her. With dripping hands at her side, she stood and walked to the cabin. Once inside she shut the cabin door, leaned against it, and heaved a heavy sigh.

God, she was *such* a wimp!

Holly dried her hands on her shirt, and rummaged in her dry bag for a clean pullover. She pulled the soiled shirt off, then tugged the new one on over her head.

And froze. A cold, sweaty, fat hand clamped over her mouth. A piercing scream lodged in her throat as heavy arms dragged her into a greasy, perspiring, smelly body and held her captive. She clawed at those thick arms. Her assailant didn't budge. She twisted in his hold, but got nothing but a jab to her back.

Holly held her breath and let it out slowly. She relaxed, hoping her assailant would loosen his hold and she'd be able to escape.

It didn't work.

Instead, his grip tightened. She couldn't breathe. Her head spun as darkness enveloped her.

Chapter Eleven

Oh, God. The man had a gun!

Holly wished she'd taken the self-defense course she'd never gotten around to before she'd left New York. It would've come in handy right about now. His grip like steel, her assailant's gun was still pressed into her lower back as he held her against his body. His hand clamped tightly over her mouth. Holly took a deep, steadying breath through her nose. She had to find her inner "center"; a yoga technique she'd seen on an infomercial.

Focus. Think.

Now what?

There was no mistaking that cold, heavy object jabbing her spine. If she wasn't careful she'd end up like Dr. Sanchez. Or worse. Roped and tied like the *Kanamari* had done with the alligator.

The man's shallow breathing rasped in her ear. The metallic scent of fresh blood and heavy sweat was repugnant. She shivered and forced herself to breathe.

There was something familiar about her assailant's cologne. Or lack of it. She'd spent enough time around it the last few months.

Harold Bennett!

Surprised. Nervous. And angry.

Okay, so she didn't know karate, or any of the other martial arts. That didn't mean she wasn't angry enough to do damage.

Insides ready to erupt, Holly decided to kick butt and show Harold Bennett exactly who he was messing with.

She was only able to twist her head to the side for a second before he snapped it back in place. But it was enough.

Yep! Harold Bennett.

He looked pale, disheveled, and menacing. His hand was so tight on her mouth she could hardly swallow her surprise.

Gun or no gun, without giving it too much thought, Holly wedged her lips apart and attempted to take a chunk out of Harold Bennett's sweaty palm.

His cupped hand evaded her teeth effectively.

"It ain't gonna work, doll, so give it up," he rasped, his fetid breath made her stomach lurch.

She gulped down her fear.

"Think I don't know what you're playing at?" he grated. "Hold still or I'll give you the same as I gave Sanchez."

Oh, God. Her mouth was dry, her teeth ached, and her tongue stuck to the roof of her mouth.

She was going to die. And only a few yards from help.

Jake was right. She hadn't wanted to believe him, but Harold Bennett was dangerous.

She had to do something. Soon.

Holly kicked her leg back between Bennett's legs. Once again the heavy-set man forestalled her and pushed her lower body away from his. Without losing control of his strangle hold of her head and neck.

She muffled a sob.

"Stupid bitch!"

She felt a slight twinge between her shoulder blades, and the next thing she knew she was flat on the floor with Bennett's sweaty body on top of her. A warm trickle spread over her left shoulder where Bennett's arm still gripped her.

Oh. God! More blood!

Was it hers? Or his?

Nausea washed over her. She gulped back the lump of fear lodged in the back of her throat. Bennett shifted his weight and raised himself off her. But not completely. His hand came away from her mouth. She drew in a deep breath ready to scream.

Bennett jabbed the gun to her neck before she could utter a sound.

"If you so much as sneeze, cough, or wheeze, you're dead. Do I make myself clear?"

Holly tried to shake her head. It was difficult with her face smashed against the floorboards on one side and his hand pressing against the other. His thick body still lay partially on top of hers. The cold, hard steel of the gun was still pressed against her jugular.

Bennett removed his hand from her face and rolled to his knees. The gun steady, he dug it deeper into her neck. She couldn't move.

Didn't dare.

From the corner of her eye she saw the moist crimson stain on his shoulder. Thank God it wasn't hers. She easily dismissed it. Her instinct for survival far outweighed her hemophobia.

Holly quickly rose up, and instinctively swung at Bennett's oozing shoulder. He dodged her assault, grabbed her arm and twisted it behind her back before she knew what happened.

For a heavy-set man, his reflexes were amazing.

The sound of metal hitting metal rang out next to her ear as Bennett cocked the hammer of his gun. He kicked her legs out from under her. She landed prone on the floor. Again.

"Have you had enough yet? 'Cause I can keep dishing it out, doll."

Every bone in her body screamed in agony; her

muscles quivered.

Where was Indy when she needed him?

Holly didn't want to admit it, but it looked as if Jake wasn't coming to save her anytime soon. She was on her own, and her position was tenuous.

"Get up," Bennett garbled. "Slowly."

He'd knocked her down only to order her to stand? Obviously, the man didn't know what he wanted. But she wasn't about to argue.

His menacing eyes were mere slits. The gun gripped tightly in his hand followed her movements. So, okay, he had the upper hand, and an unfair advantage. Although the small handgun he held looked more like a toy than the real thing. Then she remembered what that toy-like thing had done to Dr. Sanchez.

"It has a silencer, so don't get cute. No one outside this cabin will hear a thing if I pull this trigger."

If Bennett shot her right now, right here in this cabin, in the middle of the village with everyone milling around the prone Dr. Sanchez on the other side of the compound in the pavilion, no one would be the wiser. Bennett would be long gone.

And gotten away with murder.

It was the most difficult thing she'd ever done, but she willed herself to stay calm. Trying to convince herself she could handle Harold Bennett was useless. He was too agile despite being overweight and wounded. She'd learned a long time ago that timing was everything. She'd bide her time, stay alert, and wait for the right moment to catch him unaware.

Then she'd take him down!

She didn't know how at the moment, but it would come to her. She knew it. He might be able to scare the living daylights out of her, and keep her from screaming and running for help with his gun trained mere inches from her throat, but there was no way he was going to stop her from planning her escape.

Somehow she had to let Jake know that Bennett had shot Dr. Sanchez.

"Get your backpack and any first aid supplies you've got on hand. Then head for the door. Slowly. Try anything and you're dead."

"Why are you doing this? What do you want from me? Are you upset because I didn't consider your Colombian project? Why did you shoot Dr. Sanchez? It *was* you out there all along, wasn't it?"

"You want to live, doll? Shut up and do as you're told. And don't try anything. I mean it." He wiggled the gun at her, motioning her toward the door.

Holly picked up the bag and slipped a loose strap over her shoulder.

"Hold it," he spat. "I don't give a shit if you go barefoot and cut your feet to bloody stumps, but you aren't going to slow me down. Get your shoes on, and be fast about it."

Holly grabbed Jake's backpack. If she had to put her feet back into her shoes, she wanted the poinsettia paste. She had a sinking suspicion she was going to need it.

"Good idea," Bennett said. "We might need whatever he has in there, too. I could use a clean shirt. Now put those shoes on and get moving."

The overweight toad had a very creative image of himself if he thought Jake's shirt would fit.

Holly took her time putting her shoes on. She'd be damned if she'd let Bennett see how excruciating it was to slip her blistered feet into them. He might use it against her once they got away from everyone.

No way did she want to be left stranded in the middle of the jungle.

Alone!

She tied her laces in a loose knot.

118

Think. Think. Think.

"Where are you taking me?" Holly asked, reaching for Jake's backpack again.

Where the hell was Jake?

"This isn't a social visit. Shut your yap and get moving," Bennett ordered through clenched teeth. His lips hardly moved. "We don't have all day."

Holly hefted her pack over her shoulder and handed Jake's backpack to Harold. He glared at her as if she were a mental case.

"What do I look like, a pack horse? Once we're out of sight in the jungle you can combine the two and get rid of what we don't need. Now, move it. I ain't got all day."

Like she *looked like a packhorse? The man was bigger and stronger.*

And definitely a jackass!

"If we sort everything now it won't be so heavy and I won't have to carry both of them."

He wiggled the gun at her. "Stop stalling."

She slipped Jake's bag over her other shoulder and winced. The pressure dug into her sore muscles. Who was she kidding? Her entire body ached. She had to do something soon or this madman was going to drag her into the jungle. They'd never find her. She had to think of something—fast!

Holly's reflexes kicked in. Without contemplating the repercussions she swung both backpacks wide, pivoting full circle. Both bags made a pathetic arc and missed her target by a foot.

Within seconds Bennett had her pistol-whipped up against the door. Her cheek throbbed and her head ached. Bright dots flashed before her eyes. If it wasn't for him holding her up, she'd be lying in a heap on the floor.

"Try that again and I swear I'll shoot your head off."

Bennett let go. Holly slid to the floor. He ran

across the room to the side window and looked out. Was he checking to see if anyone had heard her being slammed against the door?

Holly raised her trembling hand to her burning cheek. The bone didn't seem to be broken, but the entire side of her face was on fire. She closed her eyes and mentally sent Jake an S.O.S. She prayed his ability to read her mind on previous occasions since starting this god-forsaken adventure would work this time.

Her concentration proved fruitless, and only gave her more of a splitting headache.

Holly opened her eyes. Bennett grabbed her arm and pushed her out the door and around the corner so fast she didn't have time to think about making a run for it. Or crying out for help. This time he slammed her up against the plank-board siding out of sight of the entire camp.

The gun poked into her neck.

Splinters pierced her other cheek.

"You're not going to get away with this," she hissed, turning to face him. He pointed the gun at her mouth. The scare tactic worked. She shut up. No way was she going to let this toad know she was about to wet her pants.

She refused to show fear.

"Watch me," he ground out from between thick flabby lips; spittle hit her in the face. Holly didn't dare raise a hand to wipe it off.

He wiggled the gun toward the back of the building. Holly could only stare at him. Once they left the compound and entered the rainforest they would be swallowed up by the dense vegetation.

Bennett cocked the hammer.

Holly turned and walked into the protective cover of the jungle, her shoulders drawn back, her head held high.

"So why me?" she asked. "Why kidnap me?" She

120

challenged as he forced her ahead of him in a haphazard direction away from the village.

"You were just handy, doll. Now, shut up and keep walking."

"That's not a reason."

"To piss off your lover. Jake Daniels needs to be taught a lesson for butting his nose in where it doesn't belong."

"He's not my lover. I just met the man. He isn't going to care that you've kidnapped me."

"Don't try to fool with me. Lover or not, Jake Daniels will care. You were taken on his watch."

****

Jake knew there was no way Dr. Sanchez was going to make it. He'd lost too much blood. Both compresses were soaked through. There wasn't much more they could do for him. He needed a doctor.

"We need to get him settled for the night," Jake told Ivan and Miguel. "Is there someplace where he'll be more comfortable? Do any of these tables fold down?"

The two men looked confused.

"If we can lower one to his level, we can slide him onto it and carry him to his cabin without jarring his body."

In seconds Ivan had four men clearing a table, kicking the legs underneath it and laying it on the floor next to Dr. Sanchez. Carefully, Jake and Ivan slid the dead weight of the prone body onto the table top. The comatose man moaned in pain.

Hopefully, it was a good sign.

"His body temperature is cooling fast," Jake told the men. "He's going into shock. Quick. We need a blanket to keep him warm."

Ivan snapped an order in Portuguese. One of the old women ran to her hut. In seconds she was back with two hand-woven coverlets. Jake placed the blankets over the researcher's body. Satisfied Dr. Sanchez was secure, Jake motioned for the men to carry the make-shift gurney across the muddy compound. Sonja, a pudgy, wizened woman with concern in her eyes, took over once the researcher was settled in her cabin. She quickly ushered everyone out the door.

"Sonja will take good care of him," Ivan said.

Jake nodded, then followed Ivan back outside. He glanced over at the pavilion. The rest of the women were busy cleaning the floor and putting things in order. He was glad Holly had gone back to the cabin. He was amazed, once again, at the courage she had shown despite her hemophobia. He knew it hadn't been easy for her. Looking down at his soiled hands and clothes, he thought better of walking in on her covered in blood. She'd endured enough.

"Is there someplace I can wash?" he asked Ivan, holding his hands wide to indicate his stained hands and clothes.

"The shower. Much rain. Take path there." Ivan pointed in the direction of the houses rising up on stilts. A well-worn path led to a bamboo enclosure. "You stand. Pull rope. Much water overhead collected from rain."

Jake stood fully clothed under the spray of the shower. The cold water rinsed the majority of the blood away. At least the sight of him wouldn't send Holly into another fainting spell. Now that Dr. Sanchez was being looked after he couldn't stop thinking of her. Her being wrapped around him in that too-small pup-tent last night. The earth shattering kisses they'd exchanged only minutes before Ivan interrupted them. Damn, he couldn't wait to hold her again. Kiss her. Feel her body next to his.

All night long.

Without interruption.

Jake whistled as he made his way across the village grounds towards the cabin. Towards Holly.

He opened the door and scanned the twelve by twelve, one-room structure.

Empty!

Where the hell was Holly?

Chapter Twelve

Jake squinted, adjusting his vision to the darkened interior, then entered. No sense waiting around in wet clothes.

Where the hell was his backpack?

Where the hell was Holly's?

Is this some kind of joke? Am I in the wrong cabin?

He hung his head and shut his eyes. *What the hell is going on?* Jake opened his eyes and panned the room for their belongings. Anything to show that he was in the right cabin.

He spied the bedroll in a dark corner. He *was* in the right cabin.

So where was Holly?

His foot kicked at something, sending it skittering across the floor. Jake followed it and bent down to retrieve it.

Holly's earring.

The earring Ivan had given her before they'd left camp earlier that morning, the one that had dangled from her ear and driven him crazy all day.

There was dried blood on the earring! His chest tightened. It couldn't be!

Please God, don't let it be Holly's blood.

Going back to the spot where he'd kicked the earring, he bent down and inspected the area more thoroughly. A sticky patch of blood smeared across the floorboards.

Okay, Daniels. Don't jump to conclusions. It could be Dr. Sanchez' blood. Holly's hands had been covered with the man's blood when she'd left the pavilion. Besides, there was no other evidence to indicate a struggle had taken place.

And that didn't mean a damn thing.

Something wasn't right. He could feel it. Nothing had been right since coming to Brazil. Somehow he hadn't expected things to go this far.

Just how much money was at stake?

Derrick had some explaining to do.

He had to get a grip.

Jake pushed against the cabin door. It flew wide, banged against the outside of the building, and swung back.

And just missed hitting him in the face.

The clouds had blown off and the late afternoon sun shone against the inside of the door. Another splotch of blood.

Jake gasped.

Holy mother of God! A bigger splotch stained the inside panel.

Jake's hands fisted.

He looked down in confusion, and in the last rays of the evening sun spied an even bigger splatter of blood on the wooden steps. He hadn't seen it earlier in his haste to get to Holly. The thought of her being abducted, hurt, or bleeding to death, clouded his mind.

Jake followed the blood trail around the corner of the cabin. Dark crimson stains marked the side of the building. If it was Holly's blood, her head or face had to be cut and hurting like hell.

Jake's stomach roiled. He swallowed hard to keep the bile down.

How long had it been since Holly left the pavilion? How long had she been gone? He glanced down to look for footprints in the muddy earth. His heart-rate beat like thunder, vibrated like an earthquake in his chest.

125

Two distinct sets of deep prints were visible in the soaked soil. One large and wide, the other, slim and short.

Damn! Damn! Damn!

Holly had been kidnapped!

His mind buzzed with the thought of what she was going through. Whoever had her, had to be the same person who had shot Dr. Sanchez. From the description Miguel had given, he'd stake his life on it being Harold Bennett.

The bastard was dead-meat!

Jake clutched the feathered earring and followed the footprints straight into the jungle.

"Mr. Daniels? Mr. Daniels? Where you go?"

It took a moment for Jake to realize Ivan was calling him. He shook his head to clear his macabre thoughts.

"Someone has taken Ms. Newman. There's dried blood in the cabin, and here." Jake pointed to the dark crimson blobs on the ground. "I don't know whose blood it is, but I'm going to find out."

Ivan inspected the blood stains.

"Come. We look," he said, indicating that Jake should follow him.

Together they searched the area just inside the rainforest. Daylight was fading fast, making it harder to see in the thick vegetative growth of the jungle. The trees and brush still dripped with the aftermath of the storm.

Jake pushed back the large fronds of a giant fern and stopped. The footprints were gone. It was as if Holly had vanished off the face of the earth.

****

Light faded fast under cover of the canopy. The humidity had dropped and the air was cooling.

The dripping of the rainforest past annoying, Holly slid first one backpack, then the other off her tired shoulders. The weight of one was bad enough, but both felt as if she'd had an elephant wrapped around her neck for the past hour. Her feet protested with every step.

Thankfully, Harold didn't notice she'd been dragging the bags on the ground, leaving a trail like Hansel and Gretel. She was going to keep at it as long as her stamina permitted. Or until he figured out what she was doing.

Half an hour later they entered a small clearing that looked as if someone had used it as an overnight campsite, minus the campfire. Holly stopped, her back to Bennett. She didn't care if he shot her. Her face throbbed, her feet hurt and she was dead tired. She didn't have another step in her.

"I didn't tell you to stop," Bennett's gruff but tired voice echoed around the hollow cavern-like area. Large Kapok trees circled the circumference. It would be heaven to snuggle in between the large roots and fall asleep. Perhaps she could convince him to do just that.

"If we don't rest now, we're both going to fall over. And if you don't stop, you're going to bleed to death."

"The bleeding stopped a long time ago."

Did he think she was blind? She saw the fresh ooze. His face was pale, drawn, and his shoulders slumped. His feet had been shuffling for the past hour. His breathing was labored. Gun not withstanding, all she had to do was bide her time. Finding her way back afterward would be a snap. They'd been following the river.

"I know you've got water in those bags, so hand one over. Very careful like. No smart moves."

Holly retrieved two small plastic water bottles and handed him one.

He just stood there and looked at her as if she was a moron.

"Take the cap off. Then open one of those energy

127

packets while you're at it."

He wiggled the gun at her.

Holly wondered how she could get at him without the gun going off in her face. She took the cap off and handed him the bottle along with the energy bar.

She took the cap off her bottle and tried to take her time drinking, but the water was warm and soothing and it slid down her parched throat with ease. After half the water was gone, Holly took her time with the rest, scanning the area while she drank. Familiarizing herself with her surroundings might come in handy later.

Her heart sank.

Trees, trees, and more trees. They were surrounded by ferns, dead leaves, brush, and fallen logs. Regular rainforest stuff wherever she looked. Nothing outstanding.

Except that their trail had already disappeared.

So much for dragging the backpacks!

If they didn't deviate from their current path she would be okay. It would be a snap to follow the river back to the village.

If she ever got the chance.

Bennett threw his empty container on the ground.

Holly tried not to stare at it. He didn't realize it but he'd just left a tell-tale sign for someone to follow. A sign that they'd been there. Yes! This was better than bread crumbs or drag marks. The man wasn't as smart as he thought. If Jake and the others came looking for her—make that *when* they came looking for her—they'd find the water bottle and know they were headed in the right direction.

Things weren't so hopeless after all.

"Everything out of those bags that we don't need," Bennett ordered. "They're slowing us down. Keep the food and water."

128

He sat down on a log, keeping his eyes and gun on her.

Holly took out Jake's shirts, two pairs of his underwear—boxers—hmmm. Socks. Two pair of shorts.

"Bury them."

"What?"

"You heard me. Dig a hole and get rid of those things. And don't ask why. You're not that dumb. You know why."

"There's no shovel in these backpacks."

"So, use your hands. Now get moving."

"What if I put them behind that old tree trunk over there?"

Holly watched Bennett's eyes as he contemplated the idea. He narrowed them as if trying to figure out if she was trying to trick him.

He wiggled the gun in the direction of the fallen log.

"Bury them. Give me the first-aid kit first."

Holly dug into Jake's backpack for the first-aid kit. With her back to him she took out two aspirins for herself and slid the kit across to him. It stopped at his feet. She dragged the bags in the moist soil behind her on the way to the fallen tree trunk while Bennett tried to clean his wounds.

The gun still pointed at her.

She knelt and tapped at the decayed wood at the end of the log with her fingers. She was relieved to find the inside rotted. It gave way effortlessly and didn't take Holly long to scratch out a sizable hole in the center with a stick she found lying on the ground.

"What the hell are you doing?"

"The wood is rotten. No one will find the clothes if I put them in here."

Bennett shrugged his shoulder, winced, then went back to tending his wound.

The stick broke in two. Holly threw it to the side and reached in and pulled out a handful of moist sawdust-like matter. Manic ants ran up her arm, nipping along the way. Her hand and arms stung. Heat radiated up her arms to her neck. Stifling a scream so she wouldn't make Bennett nervous enough to shoot her, Holly jumped up and brushed them off. The ants clung to her. She waved her hand in the air and quickly dug in her backpack for the can of DEET with the other.

"What the hell's wrong with you? What are you up to now?" Bennett demanded.

"Ants. I'm spraying them with DEET."

Holly sprayed her arm. The biting stopped and the ants fell to the ground.

She sprayed her other arm, and for good measure squirted some over her head.

"The mosquitoes are awful after the rain. Here, let me spray you, too." She walked toward Harold Bennett, the can in her outstretched hand ready to attack.

"Keep your distance with that shit." He raised the gun toward her head.

She stopped. Well, hell, it had been worth a try.

"I was only trying to help."

"I don't need your help."

Jake had said the same thing when she'd sprayed him.

Where was he, anyway? Was he even out looking for her? He had to know she was missing by now.

"Don't blame me if you get bitten."

"Shut up and get those clothes hidden and let's get a move on. We ain't got all damn day."

"Where are we going?"

Bennett didn't answer. He finished his energy bar and threw the wrapper on the ground next to the water bottle. Holly couldn't believe her good luck.

The slob unknowingly was helping her leave an excellent trail for Jake to follow. She looked away, picked up her single, reorganized pack, and stood, waiting for Bennett to tell her which direction he wanted her to go next.

The gun pointed toward the river.

Holly spotted the long flatboat on the bank of the river the second they stepped out from the protective cover of the rainforest. Her heart sank.

There would be no trail to follow on the river.

Chapter Thirteen

The night rapidly descended. Finding a trail in the darkness was difficult.

"Here. They go here," Ivan called to Jake. "Come."

Jake ran to the guide, mindless of the mud he kicked up behind him.

"Here," Ivan indicated, again. "The ground. Look."

Someone had been there. The ground was scraped. Someone was dragging something heavy.

"Our backpacks! Hopefully it's slowing them down," Jake stated. "They can't have gone far. We must follow their trail."

"Forest dark. Dangerous. We go early morning."

"Morning? No! We need to go now. We'll lose time. The trail will grow cold. If it's the same person who shot Dr. Sanchez, he could shoot Holly, too."

"If he kill her, no hurry."

Jake's head shot up. Frustrated at Ivan's honesty, he wanted to tear his hair out.

The thought of Holly dead...

He didn't want to contemplate it.

"I have flashlights. We go *now!*" Jake remained adamant. *Damn!* The flashlights were in their backpacks. What the hell to do. He couldn't leave Holly out there on her own.

Yes! "Get the lanterns," he told Ivan. He headed for the lantern he'd seen hanging on the outside of his cabin. "We'll use lanterns."

"The trail, it disappears at night," Ivan said.

132

"I've got to find her." He heard the panic in his own voice. When the hell had he let Holly Newman become so important to him?

Oh, man. This wasn't a good sign.

Ivan stared at him, the sympathy evident in the guide's eyes. "Come, we go," the guide said.

He stomped back to the cabin and yanked the kerosene lantern from the hook next to the door. He reached in his shorts' pocket for the small plastic bag and pulled out a book of matches. Hands shaking, he lit the wick, replaced the globe and headed straight for the dark jungle. Before he reached the edge of the village, however, ten guides armed with lanterns joined him. Others came prepared with flashlights, probably from Dr. Sanchez' research office.

Good Lord. They were all armed with bow and arrows and small blow guns. They didn't look like a deadly force, but the blow guns alone could level a large animal with one puff of the cheek.

"We help you find the *ladyzinha*."

"*Obrigado*." Jake nodded in acknowledgement. Thank God. These people understood his concern, his *need*, to find Holly.

Jake watched in amazement as the men spread out in a single row, line the perimeter of the rainforest and proceed to cautiously enter the darkened jungle. Arms-length from each other, they spanned either side of the tracks, while Jake took his place next to Ivan.

"*Obrigado*."

Ivan nodded. "We go now."

The nighttime jungle came alive with the disturbance the men created as they methodically made their way in and around trees, brush, and fallen debris. It was slow going. The light from the lanterns barely covered the immediate area circling each man. Those with flashlights were lucky enough to see several feet further in front of them. Twice,

Jake tripped over roots hidden in the fallen leaves. Once he thought he saw a long black shape slither away from him, and always the constant rustle of the treetops reminded him that Holly had to deal with the same potential nighttime dangers. Whereas they had a large contingent of men, Holly and her captor were virtual sitting ducks. Jaguars roamed the interior at night, and although not likely to attack humans unless provoked or hungry, the smell of blood would draw them in like a bear to a honey tree.

Not to mention a handful of other predators out looking for an evening meal.

Focus, Daniels. You won't help her by falling apart now. He'd handled much worse situations then this. But, he realized, his heart had never been involved.

****

Holly stopped at the river's edge. Okay, so now he'd really have to shoot her—right here and now. Because there was no way she was getting into that boat with him. Once they left shore, their trail ended. That meant she'd be totally on her own.

Tears threatened. As much as she wanted to cry, she knew they would be wasted on this madman standing behind her.

With a loaded pistol at her back.

"Keep moving," he ordered.

Her wobbly legs protested. He couldn't make her go any farther. She had to think of something. Fast!

"No." Holly swirled around to face him, purposely not looking at the gun in Bennett's hand. "It's too dark. The sun is setting. We should wait until morning. Get some rest."

"What is this, a pity party? You think I'm stupid? I'm not falling for it. Get in the damn boat."

"No. You'll have to shoot me."

"Don't tempt me. I'll shoot you in the leg so you

134

won't get far. Just think what a tasty treat you'll make for the nipping piranha or a snapping gator as you try to drag yourself away from the river. Either way, they'll have a field day taking their time picking you apart. Of course, there's always the snakes. They might take a notion to curl around that lovely little neck of yours and give you a real big hug. Your choice, doll! What's it to be?"

Holly's fertile imagination ran amuck. He'd painted too vivid a picture of what she'd been thinking since her foray into the wilds with Jake. She didn't like the reality of it. Her shoulders slumped, defeated.

"Thought you'd see it my way. Now throw that bag in the back of the boat and get in. Real careful like. Don't try anything stupid."

Holly looked at the boat, stunned. "Where's the motor?" she asked.

"Looks like you're gonna have to paddle."

"Paddle? I've never rowed a boat in my life, never mind paddled."

It was true, even living next to Cayuga Lake in central New York, she'd always gone boating with friends. Someone else always did the paddling or rowing.

"My shoulders ache now. I can't row."

"Stop complaining and get in. In case you haven't noticed, my shoulder's been shot up and I have the gun. You row."

She got in and clasped the short hand-crafted paddle, her small hand fitting the grip. She watched Bennett quickly switch the gun to his left hand, push the boat into the water with his right, and jump in. The boat rocked dangerously. It all happened so fast the thought of jumping overboard to escape was short lived. The gun firmly affixed in his right hand once again, Harold Bennett settled in the seat, his backside hanging over the edge.

Carol Henry

"Smart girl," he warned. "Now paddle this thing across to the other side and head upstream."

"Upstream? I can't paddle against this current," she told him, incredulously.

"Paddle this thing or you're fish bait." He cocked the gun, the sound echoing like a blast in the night.

****

"Over here," Ivan shouted. "Look."

Jake held his breath as he made his way over to Ivan.

"Look," the guide repeated, holding up an empty plastic water bottle.

"They were here." Jake stated the obvious, then instructed the others. "Look around and see if you can find anything else." He turned to Ivan. "Tell them to be careful not to disturb anything. There could be other clues lying about."

Ivan nodded in agreement and issued a directive to the others. Those with flashlights came closer to the area where the bottle was discovered. After shining their lights in a circular fashion, they discovered a foil wrapper from an energy bar.

"Keep looking," Jake said, elated as he continued to comb the area. The light from the lanterns cast an eerie glow through the dark jungle.

The ground was disturbed in a haphazard fashion as if there'd been a struggle. Jake's chest tightened. His jaw ached from the pressure of gritting his teeth. An unfamiliar tiredness washed over him. He couldn't give in to his fatigue now. He needed to shake it off and think. But only chaotic thoughts of the perils Holly might be facing droned in his brain. Who had her? Was it Bennett? Had he hurt her? Where was he taking her? And why Holly?

It was fairly obvious now there was no way she was involved in their scheme. She couldn't be. His relief was short lived, however, knowing she was in danger.

Thanks to him.

The woman he'd held in his arms was real; the feelings that had flowed between them were real. She was real. And he cared about her more than he should.

And she was out there somewhere at the mercy of her kidnapper. He had to find her before something bad happened to her.

Before she ended up like Dr. Sanchez.

Jake sat down on the nearest log and lowered his head into shaking hands. What the hell was going on? How had everything gone so wrong so quickly? He shook his head and took a deep breath and spotted something white sticking out of the end of the log! He yanked at it and held it up. A white shirt?

Damn. It was his white shirt.

He jumped up and pulled at it. There was more.

He dug inside to find they'd lightened their load. Not good.

Jake looked around in time to see three lanterns dim, then burn out completely. Great. Just what they needed. They were running low on kerosene. He held his lantern up and out in front of him. He was going to keep going until his own lantern quit.

He had to find Holly.

Ivan clamped a hand on Jake's shoulder before he could take three steps.

"We find her. We find your *ladyzinha*, no?"

Jake hoped the answer was yes.

Chapter Fourteen

Try as she might, Holly didn't have the stamina to keep paddling. Every draw of the paddle stretched her muscles to the max; they quivered with the strain. Unlike regular oars of a rowboat, the short paddle required the use of both hands. Switching the single short paddle from one side of the narrow boat to the other had her ribcage protesting too. And going against the current was downright strenuous.

She was going nowhere, fast.

The clouds had blown off. The heavy humidity and mist had lifted after the rain. The cool night air refreshing, and the blessed moonlit night helped with visibility on the river. In some strange, preordained way the flow of the river, the slap of the paddle hitting the water, and the quiet of the night had a pacifying, calming affect. It gave her an inner strength and renewed resolve to focus.

Harold Bennett's head nodded from side to side. *Yes!* It wouldn't be long now before he either fell asleep or passed out. She didn't care which. Eyes glued to his silhouette against the rippling waters, she feigned paddling. The gun still trained at her chest, she held her breath waiting for his reaction.

The boat slowed.

He hadn't mentioned where they were headed, but she'd heard Ivan say something about a town called Tabatinga. It was up river on the border of Colombia. It made sense. Harold had talked about a project in Colombia. Was someone waiting for him there? And would he let her go once they got there?

138

Or shoot her like he'd shot Dr. Sanchez?

Her stomach knotted. She couldn't let that happen. She wasn't ready to die.

Past caring what dangers lurked in the jungle, Holly's biggest fear was the man sitting across from her. The man whose head just lulled forward, and whose chin just bounced against his padded chest. He'd lost more blood than he wanted to admit.

Think. She had to think. What would Jake do?

If she could only get that gun away from Harold Bennett.

But how?

His head lolled again.

Holly held her breath.

It was now or never. Her rescue lay in her own hands.

Carefully resting the paddle on the edge of the boat, she waited for Harold's reaction.

Nothing!

Yes!

She cleared her throat.

Harold didn't move.

She coughed, loudly.

Again, no response.

Harold's inert body remained slumped over like a wet sandbag.

Holly sat upright as the man's gun-holding hand slid sideways on his lap and the .38 slid from his limp fingers. And landed with a thud at the bottom of the boat.

Holy crap. The noise sounded like a tree falling in the middle of the jungle. It was loud enough to wake the dead.

She looked over at Harold Bennett and froze. She wasn't sure if it was the motion of the boat listing on the river or if he had just moved.

She counted to twenty.

The man remained motionless.

139

Holly's heart raced.

With squinted eyes trained on her kidnapper she leaned forward. Had his head just moved again? Or was she seeing things?

She stilled. Counted to twenty again.

And slowly let out the breath she'd been holding.

At last! This was the chance she'd been waiting for all night.

Except now she didn't know what to do first. She couldn't reach the gun from her position. If she got too close to Harold, he might wake up and lunge at her.

What to do? What to do?

No time to think. It was past time to act.

Instinctively she stretched her left leg out as far as she dared without knocking against his feet. She worked at snagging the gun with her toes.

Crap! Her foot didn't reach.

Frustrated at her failed attempt, she grabbed the paddle and knocked the gun to the side of the boat; the sound echoed loudly in the still, Amazonian night.

Holly sat at attention.

Harold remained comatose.

The boat listed on the river.

It was now or never!

Holly dove for the pistol. The boat rocked. She brushed against Harold's pant leg on the way back from retrieving the gun. Her heart pounded. Her head buzzed. She tried to swallow. She couldn't breathe.

Adrenalin surged through her nervous system, creating a spurt of energy that had her paddling for all she was worth. She maneuvered the boat toward the opposite side of the river—back to the side the village was on.

The side Jake was on!

The heady power of being in control added to her

renewed strength and determination. No longer fighting the current, Holly let the river carry them down stream as she tried to reposition the small boat. She carefully worked her way toward shore. It took minutes. Long minutes. Then, she quickly back-paddled to keep the boat from ramming into the embankment. She didn't want to jerk Harold Bennett awake. If that happened, all her efforts to escape would be washed ashore—pun intended. And the way her luck was running lately, all bets on her living to be a ripe old age would be off.

The one good thing she had going for her now was that she had the gun.

And Harold Bennett's rotund body remained motionless.

To hell with it! Holly let the boat slam into shore. Gun in hand, she grabbed the backpack, and jumped over the side of the boat.

Right into the cold, muddy river.

And sank.

Deeper and colder than expected, the water took her under as if she wore concrete shoes. She clung to her backpack and fought her way back up, arms and legs flailing. She cursed Harold Bennett under her breath. She spit out mud and debris from the river, then forced herself to relax. She caught her breath and tried to assimilate her surroundings. Bobbing like a fishing bobber, she let the current take her downstream away from the madman who she hoped was still dead-to-the-world in his boat. She spotted several gnarled tree roots sticking out from the embankment and grabbed at them.

And missed.

Damn!

The current bounced her against brush hanging out over the water. The cold, rapid river carried her further down stream. Holly relaxed her muscles and drifted with the flow. If nothing else, it would get her further away from Harold Bennett. She spotted more branches hanging over the water and tried to catch a hold. And failed again.

Holly made several more attempts at grabbing anything along the shoreline until she finally managed to wrap her arm around what she hoped was a long, dangling root. Her arm muscles screamed in protest as the current dragged her, pulling against her hold. Her grip was tentative at best. Changing tactics, she tried to gain a foothold in the soggy earth instead.

Pushing against the current with what little strength she had left, she dug in and pulled herself out and rolled onto the solid understory of the rainforest. And landed up against a sturdy, unyielding tree trunk with a thud. Face down, breathing in rank decay and the odor of stagnant waste, Holly flipped onto her back and took a deep breath.

God, she never wanted to smell the jungle again!

She threw the single backpack to the side, lifted herself up, and leaned against the wide trunk. She shut her eyes, exhausted.

The cool night air blew across her sopping wet body. She shivered as it penetrated her clothes, her skin. But, it was nothing compared to what she'd just endured at the hands of Harold Bennett.

She'd escaped.

But her mind reeled at the danger and daring of having pulled off such a stunt. *Romancing the Stone's* Joan Wilder had nothing on her! Now all she had to do was keep well away from the alligators.

And one step ahead of Harold Bennett.

That meant she needed to get well away from the river bed. Now. Before he regained consciousness.

Holly reached up to wring the water out of her straggling ponytail. Her cold, shaking fingers came in contact with slimy leaves attached to wet, stringy roots. Was it only yesterday that a similar incident had taken place? Only then, she'd panicked with the thought of what deadly 'thing' had attacked her? Now, she laughed at such a minor incident. She'd rather face some creepy-crawly 'thing' then to have a gun held on her by a crazed madman. She didn't know what Bennett had hoped to gain by all this, but she couldn't wait to tell Jake he'd pegged Harold Bennett correctly.

Right now she'd love nothing more than to close her eyes and give in to her exhaustion. Instead, she stood on wobbly legs. First things first. She checked the rest of her drenched and muddy body for anything else that might have attached itself to her. After a quick perusal, and confident that other than the mud caked on her legs and arms, she was good to go.

Holly ignored the grime covering her body and dove for the backpack. She needed dry clothes. And more aspirin. And salve for her blisters.

Jake had instructed her to pack everything in plastic storage bags, for which Holly now thanked her lucky stars. The backpack was made of waterproof material, but water had leaked though the zipper when she'd jumped overboard! She pulled out a couple of the individual plastic bags.

Yes! The insides were dry!

Holly quickly changed into a clean pair of undies, and slipped the long-sleeved, white cotton shirt over her head and savored the dry warmth. She donned her navy lightweight capris, wishing she'd brought longer slacks. But again, they were warm and dry. She pulled her crew socks up over her shins. Her dry sneakers were like a gift from the gods.

For good measure, she doused herself with what was left of the DEET. She'd kept a small water bottle hidden from Bennett, and had lied about there being no more energy bars. Holly pulled everything out, taking inventory like Jake had taught her. Along with the poinsettia salve, she found a book of matches in another plastic wrapper, a small flashlight—yes!—a jackknife with all kinds of blades and the first aid kit. She hated to admit it, but she wished she had more of the *Palom de leche* Jake had put in her canteen—which was now empty. She ate the chocolate bar, savoring every morsel, and washed it down with half of the water, conserving the rest for later.

Holly repacked her bag. She was ready to head back to the village.

Determined to remain positive, she took stock of her situation—she'd escaped her kidnapper, had his gun, and knew her way back to the village.

So what could possibly go wrong now? She was armed and dangerous!

And had never shot a gun in her life!

****

Thomas Grapley turned and paced across his hotel room one more time. He stopped in front of the window overlooking the gardens below, dismissed their tropical beauty, and went back to his computer. He punched in a series of numbers, and waited. Nothing! He couldn't get in. He tried his personal access code.

Again, nothing.

He jumped from the wooden chair and threw himself on the bed. The coverlet flapped up along the sides as his out of shape body flounced down on the mattress. He jabbed his forefinger and thumb against the bridge of his nose and closed his eyes. He took several deep, controlling breaths. It did nothing to clear his mind.

He stood slowly, rubbed his hands over his face then went to the coffeepot where he poured another cup of the hotel's special Colombian brew. He drank half the contents in one gulp, then slammed the cup down on top of the mahogany dressing table, ignoring the splash of hot liquid that spilled over the lip of the cup.

Thomas paced, hands balled into fists, his strides short and swift. Sweat oozed from every pore despite the cool air blowing on him from the ceiling fan.

"Why can't I get in?" he shouted.

Thomas sat down at the small table where he'd set up his laptop and tried again.

Access Denied. Check Password and Try Again.

Wiping his eyes with the palm of his hands, he hung his head for a long moment. His fists came up and banged on the table. The laptop jumped sideways.

Where's Harold? If Harold's plan had worked, he should have been back long before this. What the hell had gone wrong?

He'd waited in the hotel lobby for hours—all afternoon and evening—pretending to read a damned newspaper, of all things. But nothing. Nada. Zip. Not even Ms. Newman had walked through the damn lobby door.

Damn it, what was he supposed to do now?

The plan was for Harold to beat Daniels to the village and waylay Dr. Sanchez so Daniels couldn't double check the route. If Daniels wasn't back yet, something must have gone wrong.

If Harold had made his way to Tabatinga, and was still in Colombia waiting for a flight back to Manaus, why hadn't he called?

Thomas jumped up, grabbed his suit jacket and headed for the lobby. Perhaps Harold had left a message.

"May I help you, sir?" The woman behind the desk smiled sensuously.

145

"Yes." He smiled back. "Yes. Of course. Is there a message for me? Thomas Grapley?"

She turned to check the slots behind the reception desk. "No, sir," she said, turning back to him. "There is nothing. I am sorry."

"Could you check to see if there is something for GlennCorp? Perhaps Mr. Daniels or Mr. Bennett has received something."

Once again the young woman turned from him to check. When she did, this time he took the opportunity to lean over and check the box with Holly Newman's room number on it.

Empty!

"No, sir. I am sorry. There is nothing there as well."

Damn!

Thomas masked the tension boiling deep inside.

The desk phone rang. Thomas watched the girl hurry to answer it. He shook his thoughts aside, turned and went back up to his room.

Maybe he'd typed in the wrong code. That had to be it.

Once back inside his room, Thomas went straight to the small refrigerator and grabbed an array of miniature bottles. He downed two shots of Black Velvet and one of Bacardi Gold. He took a deep breath, sat down at his laptop, and keyed in his personal authorization codes. And waited.

Access Denied!
Shit!

Chapter Fifteen

Holly threw the backpack over her shoulder, snapped the flashlight on with her left hand, and grasped the snub-nosed pistol in her right. She was ready to face anything that had the nerve to jump out at her.

I can do this. I can do this. I can do this.

She had to! There was no one else to help her now.

Deep breaths. One foot in front of the other. You can do it, Holly. You can do it.

Pep-talk over, Holly zoomed in on the riverbank as a guide. The moonlight glistened off the streaming river. The flashlight illuminated the ground at her feet. She didn't need to be tripping over tree roots and other dangerous debris. The nighttime noises surrounded her; she wasn't alone. It was the quiet she couldn't handle. Shoulders pulled back, Holly headed toward the village.

After several miles of steadily trudging through the understory of the rainforest, Holly's feet finally protested. She found a large Kapok tree and sat next to it, then dug in her bag for the god-awful salve that had become the next best thing to a miracle. She reapplied a good amount of the putrid smelling stuff to her blisters, then sat back with a deep sigh. She had no idea how much farther it was back to the village, or how far she'd already come. It was all new territory and the terrain had been harder to navigate without a machete.

Everything looked the same. The same trees.

147

Carol Henry

The same brush. The same ferns growing everywhere. And it all felt as if it was closing in on her. She closed her eyes. It didn't help. The only thing for certain was she wasn't going to reach the village by sitting still and falling asleep. Every step took her farther away from Harold Bennett and closer to safety.

And Jake.

Lord she was beat. She closed her eyes and leaned her head against the solid trunk. She had no idea what time it was, but it was past being dark. Opening her eyes, she saw the moonlight suddenly disappear behind an ominous blanket of clouds that was moving in.

Rain. That's all she needed.

Her food supply gone, Holly took a couple sips of water. She stood and put one foot in front of the other. No way was she going to fall asleep out in the open. In the middle of the jungle. Where who knew what or who might be lurking. She hadn't paid much attention to the nighttime sounds after leaving Harold Bennett behind, but now that she was a safe distance from him, her hearing was working just fine. From the sounds of the wild things all around her, there was no way she'd be able to sleep. Her main goal now was to focus on finding her way back to the village.

She hadn't gone far, however, when she realized warm water was splashing up above her ankles. She leaned over to take a closer look. Pointing the flashlight at her feet, she gasped. She was standing in a foot of water. She pivoted, shining the thin beam of light around her. *A bog!* Great! She was standing in the middle of a bog.

Dead leaves swirled around her legs.

Oh. My. God. What else was swimming around in this tannin-colored backwash? She swallowed. Hard. How had she managed to walk into a flooded

148

bog without realizing it?

And what was swimming around in it?

Holly took a tentative step backwards and froze. What direction had she come from? Swiveling around a moment ago hadn't been a smart move. She didn't even want to think about snakes, poisonous frogs, or other small critters that might be lurking in, or near by, ready to pounce. Instead, she took a deep yoga-style breath and slowly stepped backwards. She hoped she wasn't heading toward the river.

Or deeper into the jungle.

So much for dry feet!

She reached semi-dry land. And didn't stop. She turned, made a wide arc around the bog, and circled the flooded swamp. The dark canopy made it difficult to see where she was going. The flashlight trembled in her hand.

The light dimmed.

Her stomach bunched. She kept going.

One foot in front of the other. One foot in front of the other.

The gun held tightly in one hand, the flashlight in the other, Holly determinedly trudged on through the denseness of the dark interior. Once she made it around the bog, she headed back toward what she hoped was the river's edge.

Lost, tired, and angry at Harold Bennett for kidnapping her and putting her in this predicament, Holly's sense of safety took a nose dive. Where the hell was Jake? Was he even out looking for her? Was Bennett still slumped over in the boat? Was he dead? Or was he coming after her?

She heard a twig snap. She jumped and twirled around. The fading beam from the flashlight revealed nothing!

Probably just her imagination.

She turned back around and made her way more

gingerly toward the village.

She'd only taken a few more steps when she heard it again. Something was following her.

Oh, God. Had Bennett caught up with her?

Whatever was stalking her was in for a big surprise. She drew the pistol up in front of her and stood still.

Nothing.

The jungle air cooled. Her dunk in the river and the walk in the swampy bog had lowered her body temperature, and despite her constant movement, she was cold. She shivered. She'd probably die of exposure if she didn't get eaten alive first.

She had to keep moving.

Oh, lordy. There it was again. A snap! Two snaps! The hair on the nape of her neck stood on end. She spun around.

Something or someone was out there. She was sure of it. She held the gun out in front of her, not knowing how many bullets were left in the chamber, if any. She hadn't thought to check. She didn't know how to check.

Damn it, she was going to take up target practice when she got home.

Shining the now meager light in front of her, two large menacing eyes glared back. She jumped, smothering a scream. Her hand shook. Her mind ceased to function.

She wanted to run, but her feet refused to move.

What would Jake do? Not panic, that's for sure.

Dark beady eyes remained steady, trained on her.

Low to the ground, their piercing menacing glare was suddenly followed by a low growl that echoed through the night. Holly jumped back. A chill ran through every ounce of her being.

Oh, God. Oh, God. Oh, God.

Now what?

Amazon Connection

The eyes moved lower as if crouching, ready to pounce. She knew better than to move.

Holly pulled the trigger. A silent whoosh, then a thunk.

She'd forgotten about the silencer.

The animal didn't move.

She redirected the weak beam into the animal's eyes. Instead of mesmerizing this creature it only made the animal's eyes rounder, wider, and more lethal looking!

Holly repositioned the pistol and pulled the trigger. The animal yowled, jumped off the ground, and fled into the night.

Holly turned in the opposite direction, and treading on nerves of steel that were just shy of becoming too fragile to contemplate, she trudged through the rainforest. She didn't bother to wipe the tears that streamed down her face. She'd lost all sense of which side of the river she was on, or what direction she was going.

For the second time in two days she was lost in the great Amazonian rainforest.

Only this time she was alone.

At night.

Without a map.

Without a compass.

Without any idea of what the hell to do now.

Could anything else possibly go wrong?

****

Harold Bennett's head lolled back and forth as he regained consciousness. His shoulder hurt; he was stiff and sore and thirsty. He opened his eyes, adjusting to the darkness. Disoriented, he looked around. Why was he sitting in a boat on the edge of the river? Where the hell was he? And then it hit him. Damn it to hell! Holly Newman was no longer paddling the boat upstream. In fact, Holly Newman was nowhere to be seen.

151

"The bitch!" he swore out loud. "I'll kill her!"

At least she hadn't thrown him overboard while he'd been passed out.

His gun? Where the hell was his gun?

He patted his waistband feeling for his weapon. It wasn't there. Shit! He'd been holding the gun on her the entire time. It must have slipped from his hands and fallen into the boat.

Frantically, he searched for it. Nothing!

"She's got my gun! That stupid bitch took my gun! I should've shot her when I had the chance!"

Bennett stood up, steadied himself until his equilibrium settled, then stepped out. His already ruined shoes sank in the muddy bank as he slowly moved away from the boat. Without a weapon, he reached back to grab the paddle for whatever protection it might provide. It was better than nothing.

Reaching the crest of the forest floor, a safe distance from the river, Bennett started walking slowly along the edge, the river on his right. He'd only gone a few yards when he stopped to catch his breath. He clutched his chest as a pain shot through his upper body and ran through his shoulder and down his arm. His legs wobbled.

He looked out over the river and froze. He was on the wrong side of the damn river heading in the wrong direction. He was headed back toward the village. The broad had paddled them back over to the side they'd started out on. *Damn her!*

Bennett switched directions. His feet dragged in the underbrush as he slowly followed the river in order to take advantage of the moonlight. His head was fuzzy, his body heavy as if he were carrying a ton of bricks on his shoulders. Where was the boat? He had to get back to the boat.

There was no way he was going to be able to trek all the way to Tabatinga on foot.

Amazon Connection

Bennett clutched at his chest.
And fell to his knees.

****

Jake's worst fears were confirmed. His heart raced into overdrive as he followed the guides toward the river. His lantern dimmed, emitting a tentative, pathetic ray of light. With visibility limited, he lost his footing and slipped on the muck and wet reeds on the low bank and landed on his butt with a deep grunt.

"Many foot prints." Ivan shone his dimming light along the riverbank. "They take boat. See."

Jake didn't want to see. Even in the dark it was evident that a boat had been there. Footprints were everywhere. Jake's heart slid from his throat to his feet in a matter of seconds.

"Which way did they go?" he asked, knowing it an impossible question to answer.

"They go up river," Ivan said, matter-of-factly.

It made sense. If they had gone downstream, they would have passed the village and taken the chance of being detected.

"We go back. Get boats. Go up river in morning," Ivan stated.

He hated to admit it, but Ivan was right. They needed rest. They needed to regroup. They'd have a better chance of looking for signs of Holly in the daylight. But he couldn't stand the thought of leaving Holly out there in the jungle.

Alone.

In the Dark.

With Bennett.

Morning couldn't come soon enough.

153

Chapter Sixteen

Holly woke with a start. *What was that?* She closed her eyes. Tried to concentrate. All she heard was the morning sounds of the rainforest waking up around her. Birds twittered in the trees high above. Monkeys chattered at each other as they jumped from branch to branch. She rested her head between the folds of the Kapok tree, too tired to move. The heavy scent of wet soil, decaying leaves, and humid air clung to her. The river was close by.

Her eyelids flew open. She sat up straight. "Oh, God." She'd actually spent the night in the middle of the jungle—alone!

She rubbed her sleep-drugged eyes and looked around. Everything looked the same—prime rainforest, the sun streaming down between the leaves of the canopy. She smiled. She was caught in a ripple in time—it was surreal. Clear. Sharp.

Right out of a fairytale.

And then it hit her. She'd found her way back to the spot where Bennett had forced her into the boat the night before.

Yes! It wasn't far to the village!

Yes! Yes! Yes! I did it! I survived the night!

Holly smiled. Her insides tickled with the knowledge of it.

Oh, God! Her smile faded. *Bennett!* She'd left him in the boat. Had he woken up and realized she was gone? Was he looking for her?

Was he dead?

Oh, lordy. She'd shot an animal during the

night! Or was that a dream. No! She'd actually managed to survive in the wilderness.

The sudden sound of an outboard motor putt-putting up the river grew louder.

Yes! She was about to be rescued.

She had to flag down whoever was in that boat. Holly jumped to her feet.

And fell flat on her face.

Every leg and foot muscle cried out with needle-sharp pin-pricks clear up to her hips. Gritting her teeth, she rolled over and stretched her protesting muscles. A charley-horse yanked at her left calf. She rubbed it, kneading the tight muscles and took her time standing, and carefully put weight on it. She held her breath in agony, the tightness unbending. She headed to the river on legs that wobbled and hurt and weighed a ton. Debris cluttering the forest floor didn't help.

The boat grew closer. She had to hurry.

"Hello. I'm here. Stop. Stop," she called out.

The heavy revving of the motor sped up.

And raced on by.

Holly reached the river's edge and sank to her knees.

The boat disappeared upstream around the bend.

Tears blurred her vision.

Rescue had been so close.

****

Ivan steered their outboard motorboat up river close to shore. They'd been searching for over an hour and the only thing they'd come across was an empty flatboat stuck in the reeds. Jake's spirits plummeted.

Jake's head shot up. Was that someone calling? He closed his eyes and strained his ears. But all he heard was a howling monkey screeching in the thick canopy.

Ivan slowly pushed on.

An agonizing hour later there was still no sign of Holly.

Or Harold Bennett.

Dammit! This was all his fault. He should have been more alert, especially after being stranded in the middle of the jungle. Not to mention finding Sanchez shot. Either incident should have had him sitting up and taking notice. But he'd been too...

What? Blind? Busy tending to Sanchez?

Mooning over Holly?

He wasn't used to worrying about anyone else when he worked a case. Holly was a distraction he couldn't afford. Once he'd kissed her, he'd let his defenses down. And look where it had gotten him.

Gotten her!

Damn it!

If they found her alive he vowed he'd never put her in this position again. He'd...

"Look," Ivan yelled, pointing to the shoreline. "We look there."

Jake didn't see anything out of the ordinary. A closer inspection proved fruitful. A boat had definitely been there.

"Pull in, pull in," he shouted to Ivan.

Ivan was already heading towards shore. Before Ivan stopped the boat, Jake jumped out. He sloshed through the water and paused to inspect the area.

Footprints.

But there was only one set, and they led up the small embankment into the jungle.

Jake's heart rate accelerated, his breathing short and shaky. They weren't Holly's. They were way too big to be Holly's.

"A heavy person." Ivan confirmed.

"Look around," Jake all but demanded. "There has to be another set of footprints somewhere."

"Look, you see. Only one! I am sorry."

Amazon Connection

Jake did see. But what happened to Holly? Where was she? What had Bennett done to her?

She could be anywhere!

His gut told him she was still alive. She had to be, he didn't want to contemplate any other possibility. She could have been thrown overboard. Or worse.

Stay positive.

Okay, so maybe none of his other missions involved the kidnapping of someone he was becoming more than slightly interested in. Hell—if he didn't know any better he'd think he was falling in love with her.

She'd hit him in the solar-plexus the moment he'd laid eyes on her. And it hadn't gotten any better. Why hadn't he trusted his instincts? Instincts that told him no way was she involved with Bennett and Grapley's scheme. She was an honest and caring person. A survivor. She'd proven how strong and courageous she was in the face of adversity. He didn't know of another single woman capable of dealing with the situations they'd encountered. Even when faced with her fear of blood, she'd pushed it aside and helped tend to Dr. Sanchez.

Giving up the search now was not an option.

At the crest of the short embankment he found a set of shoe prints leading back toward the village. They were too big to be Holly's. He followed them for several yards. They disappeared.

Jake got down on his haunches and spread the thick grasses aside.

"Ivan, give me a hand. I've lost the trail."

Ivan came to his side and together they searched the area.

"Look," Ivan suddenly called. "They turn back. They go that way."

Jake looked in the direction his guide pointed.

"That's in the opposite direction."

157

Carol Henry

There was no need to follow it. It wasn't Holly's.

"I'm going back to check along the river," discouraged, Jake called to the others. "If she's alive, she'll be somewhere between here and the village. She'll stick to the river and follow it back."

He hoped she had enough sense to do just that. He remembered the blood on the side of the cabin. Holly's blood. What if she was laying in the jungle and needed help?

He had to keep looking.

The terrain leveled out. Tree roots hung over the side of the swollen bank making it difficult to get too close. In several spots the water submerged even the tallest bushes. Jake waded in as close as he dared despite dreading what he might find.

Behind him, he heard the others follow. They pressed on until they came to an area where water had flushed back into the interior forming a natural bog. They circled it, Ivan leading the way.

"Tracks," Ivan suddenly shouted.

Jake ran to look. Sure enough. Small shoe prints. Traces of overturned leaves and broken twigs were slight, but evident.

"Someone has been here recently. Look. Crushed leaves and scrapes."

"Someone fall. Trip on root." Ivan stated.

"No blood. That's good." Jake sent up a hearty silent prayer of thanks. It had to be Holly's trail. There weren't many natives in these parts who wore shoes.

She was alive.

Thank God.

"No blood." Ivan confirmed. "I send men back. Get boats. They follow us by river to village. We follow trail."

Jake shook his head and followed Ivan around the flooded area, elated that at last they'd found a positive indication that Holly was okay. And heading

158

back to the village.

They followed the faint trail for several more miles only to be brought up short. A pool of blood dripped from a large fern.

Jake's heart flew to his throat. He swallowed. Hard.

"Here," he called to the others, his voice choked and strangled, constricted. "Over here."

Several guides ran to his side. Ivan put a hand on Jake's shoulder in comfort. It didn't help.

The ground was scraped. A struggle had taken place. It looked serious.

Jake shut his eyes in agony while the guides fanned out, searching.

"We find paw prints," Ivan called to him. "Big. Heavy."

"A jaguar?" he asked Ivan.

"Yes. Look."

Jake looked and cringed. Holly must have been beside herself with fear. And he hadn't been there to protect her.

Damn Bennett for dragging her off into the jungle like that. He was going to kill the son-of-a-bitch with his bare hands.

Slowly. With pleasure.

****

Holly sat at the water's edge. Even the alligator basking in the morning sun, in the middle of a mud bank just up from her didn't bother her.

"Just try it, 'ally'. I've got your number." She rested the gun on the ground next to her feet, in a direct line with the reptile. Holly cautiously dipped her tank top in the water, wrung it out and slowly washed off the mud, the grime, and her tears of frustration from being stranded—again—careful not to ripple the water. She didn't want to tempt fate. She kept her eyes on the lazy gator.

So she hadn't been rescued. Once the self pity

had run its course, and she'd given herself the pep-talk of the century, she reminded herself that she'd survived a night alone in the jungle.

In the *dark* jungle.

And she'd faced danger head on.

So what if her rescue boat had sailed on without her? She was still in one piece.

And gotten a good night's sleep!

It was going to be a snap making her way back to the village in the light of day.

Confident that she was within reach, Holly carefully soaked, then wrung out her shirt and swabbed her face again. She felt a sharp sting and almost cried out, stopping just in time. She'd forgotten about the scratches on her cheek from Harold Bennett pistol whipping her and slamming her up against the cabin. The scratches on her arms and legs she'd gotten from tripping over roots and other fallen debris had stung, but she'd seen those and was prepared. After she finished washing, she reached in her bag for the First Aid Cream. There wasn't much left after Harold had gotten his hands on it, but there was enough. She spread it on sparingly, and swallowed two more aspirin.

A twig snapped, followed by a loud splash to her right. The sound echoed around her. Holly reached for the gun.

The alligator was gone.

Ready or not, it was time for her to go, too. She picked up her backpack and swung it over her left shoulder, pistol in her right hand, and headed back to the village.

It took her longer than anticipated to reach the village, but this time she made it without incident.

When she saw the first building on stilts, she sent up a prayer of thanks. New tears, this time tears of joy, formed. She didn't bother to brush them away.

Amazon Connection

Her harrowing adventures were over.

The children spotted her first. They ran back to the compound to tell the others. Holly had just enough time to tuck the gun in the bottom compartment of her bag before they returned. She found herself surrounded by half-naked excited children and was immediately caught up in their laughter. They trailed behind her as they made their way toward Sonja and Pilar, who were now waiting for her at the crest of the bank.

"Your man, he and Ivan go look for you," Sonja told her, a large smile on her sun-kissed, wizened face. Her body was covered with a loose-fitting, bold floral print dress that flowed down to her ankles. "They come back soon."

"Come. You eat." Pilar pointed toward the pavilion. Like Sonja, she was also dressed in a flimsy sack-like dress with wild colorful swirls throughout. Their handcrafted jewelry, long dark hair, and smooth olive skin were strikingly exotic.

"*Obrigada*," Holly said, overjoyed by their warm reception. She was starved. And exhausted.

****

Jake and Ivan followed Holly's trail. It led right back to the spot where they'd lost her trail the night before. This time when they searched the water's edge, they picked up her tracks leading back toward the Village.

She was okay. Jake smiled, sent up a silent prayer of thanks, and gave Ivan a thumbs up. Together they made their way along the river's edge.

The morning sun seemed a bit brighter, the clouds had vanished, and the rainforest was definitely a happy place. The last puffs of steam rolled off the river and hung in the canopy.

He couldn't wait to hold Holly in his arms.

Immediately upon reaching the village Jake ran to the cabin. He threw open the door and took only a second to adjust to the dimness of the darkened room. Yes! She was there. Asleep on their bedroll.

Thank God!

Jake rushed to Holly's side and knelt beside her. Her beauty grabbed at his heartstrings. The early afternoon sunlight filtered through the open window, shining down on her like a beam from heaven above. Her hair lay splayed across the small red camping pillow. A multicolor, silk sarong gently caressed her body as it twisted seductively around her long, tanned legs. His heart knotted. He could hardly breathe.

And then he saw the bruise on her pale cheek, and the scratches on the other side of her face and arms. His chest tightened.

Harold Bennett was definitely a dead man!

He tenderly traced a path across her cheek with his shaking fingertips. He brushed the loose strands of her angel-soft hair aside. The urge to lie down beside her took over, and he slid in next to her and gently gathered her in his arms. She stirred and leaned into him.

He tightened his hold.

God! He was in heaven. He wanted nothing more at this moment then to make love to this brave, brave woman. But she'd been through too much trauma and needed her rest. She'd been kidnapped at gun point, and left to fend for herself in the rainforest. At night. In a dense jungle. With God only knew what lurking around every tree!

Good God! She'd had to deal with a jaguar!

He had to remind himself that she had survived. On her own. He'd underestimated her from the very beginning. But no longer.

There was no way she was involved in Bennett and Grapley's scheme.

No way!

Jake brushed her bangs aside and reverently

Amazon Connection

kissed her forehead despite the non-reverent feelings coursing through his humming body. He let the kiss linger, enchanted by the exotic smell of her—tropical herbs and spices. He covered her face with feather-light kisses, her temple, her eyes, her cheek, her nose. She moaned softly. Sensually.

Her eyes fluttered open.

"Jake," she whispered. "Am I dreaming?"

"I'm here, Sweetheart. It's no dream. I'm here."

"Hold me, Jake. Just hold me."

"No problem."

They clung to each other, neither speaking for long moments. But with her body wrapped so tightly against his, his need to be closer, much closer, took over. Before he could stop himself, he was raining kisses all over her face. Again.

Holly squirmed seductively against him. Her lips met his. Within seconds they clung to each other in a hold that knew no bounds. Their tongues tangoed to a rhythm only the two of them heard and responded to. The dance was as exotic as the tropical rainforest.

Coming up for air, they looked longingly into each other's eyes, saw the shared desire, and dove in for another long, satisfying kiss.

"Jake. Oh, Jake," Holly moaned, trying to catch her breath.

Jake gave her only a moment before he slid under the covers with her and they frantically removed each others clothes. He kissed her again, this time slow, lingering. Her warm, naked body melted against his. He ran his hands over her back, her bottom, and pulled her tight up against him.

She fit perfectly.

She didn't resist. He felt her breasts rub up against his chest and he came undone. He didn't want to rush things. He wanted to enjoy every inch of Holly Newman.

163

Carol Henry

Every delicious inch of her.
Inch by sexy inch!

Chapter Seventeen

"You were right all along, Jake. It was Bennett. He was waiting for me when I came back to the cabin. He held a gun to my head. There was no way I could yell for help."

"God, Holly, I'm so sorry," Jake breathed, holding her close as they lay propped up against the wall, his arm protecting her from the rough boards. "I went crazy worrying about you out there alone in that jungle last night. When I discovered you were missing I went berserk. I blame myself for everything."

Jake had all to do to keep his desire for her in check, especially after having just made love to her. His heart was still beating erratically. His desire for her hanging by a thread. He looked into her crystal green eyes and smiled, pleased at the sparkle he saw shining back at him. He couldn't believe she was actually safe.

And in his arms.

"Bennett didn't...?"

"I'm fine, Jake. Honest."

"I'll kill him if he did. I swear, Holly, if he laid a hand on you..." He squeezed her shoulder, her skin smooth and enticing.

"He threatened, but he didn't. He was wounded. Apparently Dr. Sanchez had a gun, too and shot back."

The thought of Bennett shooting Holly like he'd shot Dr. Sanchez made Jake's insides boil.

"If it wasn't for him holding a gun on me the

entire time, I would have escaped sooner. The gun had a silencer on it. I couldn't take the chance he'd shoot me and no one would hear. The thought of some wild animal finding me and finishing me off kept me and my feet on the move."

"How did you manage to get away from him?"

"Once we got in the boat I almost gave up hope of anyone ever finding me alive. But I could see it wouldn't be long before he gave out. He'd lost a lot of blood and was getting pretty weak from all the walking we'd been doing. So I waited. When he finally passed out, I paddled for all I was worth to the riverbank. I took his gun and slipped over the side of the boat."

"That explains why we only saw one set of prints leading into the rainforest."

"His shoulder's pretty shot up so there was no way he could paddle the boat. He must have woken up and decided to go the rest of the way on foot. I don't think he'll get far." Holly snuggled up against Jake, and took a deep, steadying breath. "After I jumped out of the boat, the current carried me downstream. It took several tries, but I was finally able to grab hold of some tree roots hanging over the water's edge. I kept close to the river until I came to a bog. Then I had to go around it, deeper into the jungle. It was so dark I had a hard time finding my way. Then the flashlight started to go dim."

"God, you must have been petrified. Dammit, Holly, I'll never forgive myself for this."

"Stop beating yourself up, Jake. If you remember, I insisted that I was going to follow you into the rainforest." She patted his chest and rubbed her fingers down his mid-section.

She was treading on dangerous ground, touching him like that.

"There was no way you or anyone else was going to keep me from following you. You were trying so

Amazon Connection

hard to make me change my mind, I had to find out what you were keeping from me." Holly smiled and snuggled closer. "I think there's plenty of blame to go around. And besides, I survived."

"Thank God! You didn't need me after all."

"I wouldn't say that. There were a few times I cussed you out while I was floundering around out there. But there were more times when I'd asked myself what you'd do. I didn't have time to think about the dangers, just how to deal with them. When I heard your boat go by this morning, I almost lost it."

"You were there? You heard us?" Jake turned to her in surprise. "I'm so sorry, Holly. I thought I heard someone call out."

"Yes." She smiled up at him. "I was devastated. I was so sure I was about to be rescued. I knew I wasn't far from the village, and it was only a matter of time before I made it back. Knowing you were looking for me gave me strength to keep going. I couldn't wait to tell you that you were right about Harold Bennett."

Jake pulled her close, and kissed her fiercely.

After several satisfying and breathless moments later, Jake pulled back and tucked her into his shoulder. He had things to tell her. Things that weren't going to be easy.

"We didn't find Bennett." He didn't want to alarm her, but she had to know the truth. The man was still out there. "His trail started to head back to the village..."

"You mean he really was coming after me?"

The alarm in her voice jabbed at his chest.

"Relax, Sweetheart, for some reason he turned back around and headed upstream along the river where his trail led deeper into the jungle."

Holly reached up and laid her hand on his cheek and turned his lips to hers. And kissed him tenderly.

167

Carol Henry

"Thank goodness," she breathed next to his lips. "I was so worried. It kept me going. That and thinking of you."

He took advantage of her lips so close to his and kissed her, deeply.

"We decided not to follow his tracks. Our main concern was finding you. When we get back to Manaus I'll alert the authorities, let them handle it."

She reciprocated his kisses, their lips playing an erotic dance with each others.

"God, that man is crazy," he sighed, releasing her slightly.

"He's probably out there looking for Tracker."

"Tracker! Damn. That's the guide who stranded us to begin with." Jake sat back and banged his head on the wall. "Bennett must have paid him a pretty penny to double cross us. I can't wait to nail him. The sooner he's behind bars, the better."

"I have his gun."

"I thought so. We found your footprints and a couple of shell casings. I've got to tell you, Sweetheart, it gave me a scare. What you must have gone through last night..."

She snuggled closer, her breasts rubbed against him.

It was a good thing he was already laying down.

"I'm safe," she whispered, and wrapped her smooth arms around him.

He moaned, and rubbed his hand up and down her arm. He cupped her chin then tilted her face to his. She met his lips in a searing kiss that almost drove him deeper over the edge. He released her long enough to look deep into her sparkling sexy, green eyes that would forever remind him of the tropical rainforest.

"I am so proud of you, Holly."

Holly kissed him, slowly, hungrily, confidently this time. "I could stay like this forever," she finally

168

sighed. She laid back down, pulling him with her.

"Me too." Jake barely managed. He didn't resist.

He still had to tell Holly about Bennett and Grapley's scheme to incriminate her. And that he had suspected her of being involved. If he wanted any kind of a relationship with her, which he did, it had to be built on trust.

But it would have to wait until later.

Much later.

****

It was damn hard leaving Holly so soon after the incredible hours they'd just shared making love, but he needed to get back to work.

He needed to check on Dr. Sanchez.

Despite the evidence that Bennett had shot Sanchez, and that Holly had the gun to prove it, he still needed to check the pipeline route to confirm that the two men had tampered with the maps. They were definitely involved in money laundering from the corporation. And, if he could find the bullet that ripped through Dr. Sanchez's chest, all the better. It would seal Bennett's fate.

No way were they going to make it back to Manaus in time to sign contracts. If they made it back late Saturday, they'd be lucky.

Jake reluctantly disentangled himself from Holly's warm, sexy, sleeping body, got dressed, and headed for the pavilion where Ivan and the others were already gathered.

"*Ladyzinha*, she is resting?" Ivan asked, as Jake sat down next to him.

Pilar and Sonja served him a hearty dish of plantains, meat and rice. Jake was more than happy to dig in.

"Yes. She is safe and resting. Thanks for your help."

"We go look for that man, Bennett?"

"No. I'll contact the police when we get to back

169

to Manaus. The authorities will take care of him soon enough. How is Dr. Sanchez? Can he be moved yet?"

Ivan had gone to check in on the researcher while Jake had looked in on Holly. Even now he wanted to run back to the cabin to be by her side; to make sure she was still safe. That Bennett wasn't coming after her again. But he knew he was being ridiculous, letting his emotions for her get in the way.

"Sonja say he better. They take him to doctor in boat."

Jake hoped they hadn't waited too long; the man had lost a lot of blood.

"Do you have access to Dr. Sanchez' maps?" he asked Ivan. "I still need to check the pipeline route. Find where Dr. Sanchez was shot. Can you take me?"

"Yes. We eat. Then go." Ivan smiled and resumed eating.

Jake was sorry to have missed Dr. Sanchez before they had taken him away. Thankfully the man was doing well. Hopefully, he would make the boat ride to Tabatinga. If he died, Bennett would add murder, as well as kidnapping, to his list of crimes. As much as Jake wanted Bennett on any count he could get him on, he didn't want to see an innocent man die.

Ivan pointed to the cabin he and Holly shared. Two large men stood guarding the front of the building. Two lounged against the back.

"*Obrigada*," Jake nodded to Ivan, pointing at the men. "*Obrigada*."

He didn't think it likely that Bennett would try anything again, but he would rest easier knowing someone was there while he checked out the route with Ivan.

Jake joined Ivan at the far end of the village

Amazon Connection

compound, and together they headed out to the field. They'd gone about two miles when they came to a patch of blood-stained dirt

"Too much blood. This must be where Miguel found Dr. Sanchez."

"Yes. Blood over here." Ivan pointed.

"Bennett's. Not as much blood. He couldn't have been hit very hard. That accounts for him being able to make it back to camp and kidnap Holly."

Just thinking about Holly being taken against her will, the bruises on her cheek, sent chills down his spine, again. He had to keep reminding himself Holly was safe and resting back at the village under the security of blow-dart wielding native guards.

"The bullet went straight through Dr. Sanchez, so it must be here somewhere," Jake told Ivan, who was already searching along the side of the rutted roadway.

The two men scanned the area

No luck.

"You stand here." Jake motioned for Ivan to stand where Dr. Sanchez had probably stood. "I'll stand over here. You look behind me. I'll check things out behind you; see if we can find anything we can use as evidence."

They exchanged places and carefully combed every inch of ground and shoulder-height brush close by. It took ten minutes, but Jake finally hit pay dirt.

"I've got something."

Ivan rushed to his side.

"There's a bullet lodged at an angle in this tree. Let me see your machete."

Ivan handed him the machete. Jake hacked away at the small tree above the bullet. The top of the tree fell over. Jake then cut underneath the bullet. An eight inch section broke free. Jake held it up in triumph.

"This should work. I'm sure the bullet has

171

Harold Bennett's fingerprints all over it."

Ivan nodded, and smiled.

"Let's finish checking the map. I have a feeling it won't take long."

In companionable silence the two men moved on. They followed the field planted in banana and pineapple, with a few squash on the side. They stayed to the edge of the cropping system until they came to a manioc grove. They veered left and entered the rainforest. The shade of the trees blocked the hot afternoon sun. Jake checked his map, made a few notations, then nodded for Ivan to continue on.

"Come," Ivan said. "We go above trees. You see far."

Ivan led him through a series of stations where they rappelled high above the canopy. Before he knew it, they'd covered a significant amount of the area. As predicted, Derrick was right—the map Bennett and Grapley presented had been falsified. As much as he was enjoying the spectacular view above the lush Amazonian rainforest in varying shades of rich greens as far as the eye could see, he had all the proof he needed. And the bullet from Bennett's gun.

"We can go back now," Jake stated, closing his notebook. "You've been very helpful, my friend. How can I ever repay you?"

"There is no need."

Confident that he had all the ammunition needed to convict Grapley and Bennett, Jake was only too glad to head back to the village.

And Holly.

Holly was sitting in the pavilion with Pilar when he returned. As soon as she spotted him she jumped up and flew into his arms and kissed him.

"I wasn't dreaming was I? You. Me. The cabin?"

"You. Me. Definitely." He couldn't hide his grin.

172

"Where'd you go? I was worried when I woke and you were gone. Pilar only said that you'd be back soon. I couldn't understand anything after that."

"Ivan took me to finish checking the pipeline route. We found the bullet from Bennett's gun." He held the twig up for her to see.

"What about my fingerprints on the gun?"

"I don't think that will be a problem, Sweetheart. I'm sure Bennett's fingerprints are all over this bullet. You won't have to worry about him any more.

She sighed and wrapped her arms through the crook of his. Together they headed for their cabin.

Jake prayed he was right.

Chapter Eighteen

"Are you awake?" Holly whispered in Jake's ear, tickling it with her index finger to make sure he was, in fact, awake.

"I am now," he whispered, pulling her into his arms and kissing her.

It had rained through the night, but the Amazonian rainforest woke to another warm, humid, sunny morning. Holly was still floating on air with the afterglow of having made unbelievably satisfying love.

All night long.

With Jake.

She cuddled, warm and sleepy in his arms.

"Come on, sleepy head. It's going to be a long day," Jake said. "If it wasn't for the roads being washed out with all this rain, we'd be back in Manaus by now. I only hope they got Dr. Sanchez to a doctor in time."

They were both quiet for a moment, each thinking their own thoughts about the chaos Bennett had inflicted and the disastrous outcome Bennett and Grapley's route would have caused to the indigenous people and the environment.

"It's a long boat ride to Tabatinga," Jake finally broke the silence. "Are you sure you're up to it this morning?" Jake tucked her head against his shoulder.

"Hmmm. Right now I don't care if we ever leave." She purred as she ran her fingers down his chest, brushing through the springy hairs.

Amazon Connection

"If you don't stop that, you'll get your wish. But unless you want Ivan or one of the others to walk in on us, we'd better get a move on."

Jake gently kissed her forehead then rolled out of their bedroll onto the floor.

"Come on woman; get dressed so I'm not tempted to take you back to bed. Pack those bags and let's go find something to eat."

Holly stood, a warm tingle coursing through her. She wished they had more time.

After a breakfast of fresh fruit, rice and coffee, Ivan and two of the guides prepared the boats. Children gathered around with their pet lizards, sloth, and monkeys to wave them off. It was rather festive and Holly felt as if she was leaving many friends behind.

"Ivan says we can catch a small plane in Tabatinga back to Manaus," Jake said. He placed his hands on her shoulders as she settled in the seat in front of him. She placed her hands over his in acknowledgment of their shared new-found love.

It was a tranquil, romantic ride. Holly's rose-colored glasses were firmly in place as their boat meandered towards their destination.

With renewed hopes and dreams for the future, Holly's happiness overflowed like the river itself during the rainy season. She closed her eyes, contemplating being held in Jake's arms once again. Now she understood her sister's excitement over marrying Randy. She hoped she made it back in time for their wedding. William Randall Huntington, III's family was footing the bill and it was going to be a doozy of a wedding.

Her sister would never forgive her if she missed it.

She didn't want to miss it.

The sun sparkled off the river, the lush tropical rainforest greener, the sky cloudless.

175

The boats rounded another bend in the winding river, Holly spotted the spectacular colorful clay-cliff. In a frenzied commotion the sky suddenly filled with the bright psychedelic colors of indigo, turquoise, violet, various stark shades of green, golden honey, and reds. Hundreds of macaws took flight.

The strong pull of the macaw's commitment for each other, and the affinity with them struck deep in Holly's heart. An omen for sure. She planned to spend the next fifty plus years with Jake. She squeezed Jake's hand. In silence they watched the myriad of colors overhead. He returned the squeeze, silently acknowledging the passions they'd shared yesterday and last night.

Words weren't necessary.

Tears of happiness filled her eyes. Her spirits soared with the birds. Nothing could ever burst the bubble surrounding her heart. Despite all that had happened out here in the jungle, she'd finally overcome her fears.

And fell in love!

It was time to finally put it all behind her. Her new found confidence was liberating. She could trust in love again.

Thanks to Jake.

Several hours later they arrived at the small wooden docks of Tabatinga. Ivan escorted them to a small outdoor café where they ordered a cold drink and a bite to eat.

"I make arrangements for plane to take you to Manaus," he said, then turned and walked down the narrow road that lead to an unpaved side street.

They were just finishing their light meal when Ivan returned.

"I'm sorry. The plane will not be ready until afternoon."

"Is there any word on Dr. Sanchez?" Jake asked.

Amazon Connection

"He is not doing well. He is being cared for. There is rainforest reserve not far from here; you walk high on bridge above trees. I show you."

"It's a different world up there," Jake turned to Holly. "You'll love it."

"It was cloudy when I flew into Manaus. I wasn't able to see the rainforest. I was hoping I'd get a chance to do this before I left, but I've been so busy with the project I didn't have time."

"Then I'm glad Ivan suggested it. We have time now."

Twenty minutes later Holly and Jake were walking across the aerial bridge high over the emergent layer of the rainforest.

"This is magnificent," Holly whispered as they stopped to observe the tops of the trees for miles in either direction.

"Look," Jake pointed to a large decimated area that had been laid bare by clear-cutting. "It's more obvious when you can see it from this angle. When you're on foot, it isn't near as dramatic."

"I can see both sides of the picture, now, but it's still sad."

"Progress," Jake shook his head.

"I'm glad GlennCorp is concerned enough to utilize the land already decimated by that kind of progress," Holly said. "Except for that eyesore, the rest of this panoramic view is spectacular."

Jake agreed. He kissed her forehead, then put his arms around her waist and they continued walking across the swinging bridge, arm in arm.

"Once this is over we'll have more time together."

"I'm looking forward to it," she replied.

"Ever been to Alaska?" he asked.

"No. Do they have alligators there?"

"No. Just bear and moose. And the best salmon and halibut you've ever tasted."

177

Holly's eyes grew round.

Jake chuckled. "Don't worry, we'll handle that hurdle when the time comes. As soon as we get back to Manaus I'm afraid I'll be busy cleaning up this mess."

"Yes, I have a few phone calls to make, as well. My sister is probably going to wonder what's become of me when I don't show up tomorrow at her bridal shower. Plus, it's my mother's birthday. Neither one of them is going to forgive me for ruining the big event."

Together they stared out over the varying shades of the tropical greenery in front of them.

"I'm sorry you missed your flight, Holly. Family is important. You should be there with them."

"What? And miss the adventure of a lifetime? You've got to be kidding," Holly smiled up at him. "Really, Jake. I'm not just saying that. Surviving out here on my own taught me a lot about myself. I've been afraid of things my whole life and have worked hard at trying to overcome them. I can deal with anything nature wants to throw my way, now. As long as I'm prepared and stay calm."

"That's my girl."

Holly turned into his arms and he lowered his head, his lips finding hers. The kiss was long and tender. Holly's toes curled.

"You didn't need protecting at all, Sweetheart." He smiled down at her. "You did fine all by yourself."

"You were beside me all the way, Jake. Not to mention I had Bennett's gun. I hope they catch him."

"Not to worry. They will."

"What about Thomas? Do you think he's involved as well?"

"Without a doubt. Grapley is the computer guru, so he's in it up to his ears, too. As soon as we get back to Manaus I'll contact Mr. Delgado and straighten everything out. Don't worry, we have all the evidence we need to nail both of them," Jake assured her, checking his watch. "It's time to head back. We don't want to miss the plane. God only knows when the next one is scheduled to depart."

The plane turned out to be no bigger than a gnat. Holly's heart fell to the ground with a hearty thump. She swore the boat they'd traveled in that morning was a better bet at getting them back to Manaus in one piece than this rattle-trap.

"It is safe, I am assured." Ivan tried to convince them.

Her heart wedged firmly in her throat. So much for her new found confidence.

"Come on, Holly," Jake said, pulling her toward the plane. "You survived the jungle on your own, you can survive this. I'll be right beside you."

"If that plane goes down and kills us, Daniels, I'll never forgive you or speak to you again."

"It won't. If Ivan says it's safe, I believe him."

Jake helped Holly into the single engine plane. It coughed and sputtered, then coughed again as the ragged looking propellers started twirling. The churning noise made speech impossible. Holly gripped Jake's hand. She hung on all the way to Manaus.

When they landed and exited the belly of the loud monster, Holly thought she'd never be able to hear again. But by the time they reached the hotel, her eardrums had recuperated and her legs had stopped shaking.

Jake escorted her to her room.

"I'll order room service as soon as I get back to my room."

"That sounds lovely."

Jake leered at her, wiggling his eyebrows, his sexy smile making her heart do flip-flops.

"In the meantime, I have a few phone calls to make. I'll be back as soon as I finish. We'll have the

Carol Henry

rest of the night to ourselves."

The anticipation of making wild and passionate love with him again had her heart racing.

"I know you can take care of yourself," Jake said, taking the key-card from her and inserting it into the security lock. "But humor me while I make sure your room is safe before I leave you here alone."

Jake checked behind the curtains, the doors, under the furniture, then did the same in the bathroom.

"You don't think..."

"Harold Bennett? Or possibly Thomas Grapley? Hopefully Bennett's lost somewhere in the middle of the rainforest trying to get to Tabatinga."

"He might be dead."

"We don't know that. And until we do, we have to be careful. His guide might have picked him up and taken him to a doctor."

Holly shuttered, her eyes wide.

"Lock the door when I leave. Do not open it for anyone other than room service. Or me. Check through the peephole. Make sure it isn't Bennett, or Grapley."

"Grapley...?"

"Yes. Grapley. Don't argue with me, Holly. I have to go. I want you to be here when I come back."

"Yes, sir." Holly saluted.

Jake didn't laugh.

"It's not funny, Holly. We don't know what those two are going to do next. I'm not sure about Grapley, but Bennett knows he's screwed. Which makes him even more dangerous if he shows up. Hopefully, he's still somewhere in the middle of the interior and hasn't had a chance to contact Grapley. I'll alert the authorities as soon as I get back to my room."

He pulled her into his arms and kissed her like there was no tomorrow. Her toes tingled, not to mention other parts of her body.

180

"Don't go anywhere. I don't want you wandering around without me until this is settled. I'll meet you here."

He leaned in and kissed her, then turned to leave.

Holly followed him to the door and watched as he back-tracked down the outside corridor. Her hand on her lips savored his touch.

"Stay inside and lock that door," he called to her over his shoulder, not turning around as he continued to his own room.

Holly shut the door and locked it. Until they knew where Harold Bennett and Thomas Grapley were, she knew they needed to be cautious. She didn't think Thomas posed a threat, but then she hadn't expected Harold to turn out to be a murderer or a kidnapper, either.

Glad to be back in one piece, she wanted to keep it that way. Happiness bubbled deep inside as she contemplated lying in Jake's arms later tonight.

After a quick shower Holly applied antiseptic cream to her cuts and scratches then slipped into a loose-fitting sundress. Her skin had become sun-bronzed from her time in the Brazilian sun so she didn't need make up. Still, she applied enough to cover the bruises on her cheek. She blew her hair dry and let it fall against her shoulders. She slipped into a comfy pair of strapless sandals. Settling in the cushioned wicker chair she reached for the phone.

It was time to call her sister to apologize and explain why she wouldn't be able to attend the bridal shower. Her mother was next. She promised them both that she would be at the wedding and that she'd make it up to them when she got back home.

She kept her mishaps in the dark, scary jungle, especially the part about being held at gunpoint by Harold Bennett to herself. She almost mentioned Jake, but something held her back. She couldn't wait

Carol Henry

to tell either of them, but she wanted to tell them face to face. After her last disastrous relationship, she'd sworn off men and they'd believed her.

Besides, she didn't want her good news to detract from her sister's wedding.

About to call Marcia at Wild and Wonderful and fill her in, Holly jumped at the loud knock at the door. Certainly it couldn't be Jake already. She hadn't spent that much time on the phone.

Holly put the phone down and cautiously made her way to the door. She looked through the security hole. Tall, handsome, and sexy as all get out, his dark hair still damp and clinging to his forehead, Jake Daniels looked good enough to eat.

Holly stepped back to unlatch the lock, then couldn't resist taking another look at Jake though the security window. This time she looked at his lips in anticipation of them sliding over her own lips.

And stopped. Those lips weren't smiling. They were thin and drawn. She looked up into his eyes and froze. His eyes were drawn and pensive.

Something was wrong.

She did a quick check around him just in case.

Nothing.

Nothing but the lush tropical vista behind him that she'd become accustom to every time she opened her door.

Holly slid the lock loose and opened the door. About to fly into Jake's arms, his hands grasped hers instead. She frowned.

He pushed her from him, and frog-marched her backwards into the room.

His touch rigid. His smile missing.

Had she done something to upset him?

"Jake. What is it? What's wrong?

"Hello, Mz. Newman. Long time no see." Thomas Grapley swung from around the outside of the door, gun in hand. He nudged Jake into the room, and kicked the door shut with his foot.

Chapter Nineteen

"Sorry, Sweetheart, bad luck seems to dog our heels," Jake said, keeping his eyes on Thomas Grapley.

For once there was no sign of Jake's poker face. Instead, his eyes were full of concern. And regret?

Holly threw her arms around his neck and pulled him to her.

Despite the gun Thomas was pointing at them, she buried her face in Jake's chest. Her heart pounding along with his, he hugged her, fiercely.

Tears threatened.

"Where's Harold?" Thomas snarled from behind them. "What did you two do with him?"

"What do you mean, where's Harold?" Jake asked, as if he had no clue Harold had followed them into the rainforest.

Apparently Thomas was unaware of Harold's escapades. Which meant Harold hadn't made it to Tabatinga.

"Don't be stupid," Thomas snapped. "You know as well as I do that he followed you on your so-called 'expedition'. So cut the crap. Where is he?"

Hopefully stranded in the middle of the Amazonian wilderness.

What an ironic twist of fate. Harold had worked so hard to keep them from reaching the village by leaving them stranded. Now he was the one stranded.

"I don't know where Bennett is," Jake continued. "If he did follow us into the jungle, he must still be there. I haven't seen him."

Holly knew Jake was used to men with guns and could probably disarm Thomas before he even thought about pulling the trigger. Maybe telling half-truths would buy them time. But, after her ordeal with Harold Bennett, she wasn't so sure.

"Listen, Tom, this is about being passed over for that promotion, isn't it?" Jake tried to keep Thomas talking. "Your beef isn't with Holly. Why don't you let her go?"

"Like that's going to happen. Sit down. I want some answers."

"What do you want to know?" Jake asked, his voice quiet, slow.

"What did you do with Harold?"

"I told you, I haven't seen him," Jake said.

Holly watched as Thomas' left eye twitched.

Not a good sign.

"Don't bullshit me," he stuttered. "I know something happened out there. He was supposed to be back yesterday and I haven't heard from him. So what gives?"

"I told you..."

"Yeah, yeah, you haven't seen him."

Holly saw the look in Thomas' eyes and knew he was about to go headfirst over the edge. She'd seen the same look on Bennett's face when he'd kidnapped her.

Thomas raised the pistol. His grip tightened.

How had she missed this flaw in their personalities? She'd worked beside them on and off for three months. They were sleaze-balls, yes, but she'd had no inkling they were capable of murder. In fact, she hadn't even known they'd carried guns.

Chills ran through her just thinking about having spent so much time with both of them. Had she really been that naive?

"Harold hasn't contacted you yet?" She pulled

herself together and asked, trying to keep her voice calm, following Jake's lead to stall for time.

"You know damn well he hasn't or I wouldn't be here questioning you, now would I?"

"There is any number of things that could have happened to him out there in the wilds," Holly said. "Why, our own guides left us stranded and we had to find our way to the next station on our own." Holly tried to make it sound like an every day occurrence so Thomas would calm down.

"That's right. It's a jungle out there," Jake said, tongue in cheek. "Anything can happen."

It was a risk, but Holly hoped the distraction would give Jake enough time to figure something out.

Anything.

Like now!

Thomas pulled the hammer back on the gun.

Dear God, she'd come to recognize and hate that sound. Thomas waved the snubbed-nose pistol in circles between them. She shut her eyes, trying to keep from freaking out.

"Cut the bull," Thomas demanded.

Holly opened her eyes to see Thomas Grapley's eyes grow bigger and rounder than she'd ever seen anyone's. He nervously stepped from foot to foot, the grip on the gun becoming more precarious.

"You want to know what happened?" Jake asked, barely keeping control of his voice. "I'll tell you. Once the authorities catch up with him, he's going away for a long time. He shot Dr. Sanchez and kidnapped Holly. You don't want to follow in his footsteps, do you, Tom? You don't want to be arrested for attempted murder, too."

Oh, my God. What was Jake doing? His change in tactics had her mind reeling. Couldn't he see that Thomas wasn't in his right mind? Jake's semi-calming tone didn't have the desired results he'd

Amazon Connection

anticipated; in fact, it had the opposite as far as Holly was concerned. She stepped forward to add her plea to Jake's. Jake put his arm out to stop her.

"Put the gun down, Tom. The most you'll be accused of is attempted money laundering. You don't want to add killing to the list, do you? Your scheme has fallen through. It's over."

Holly heard the hammer of Thomas' gun connect a split second before the shot rang out. She dove toward Jake pushing him aside. Too late, the bullet slammed into his shoulder. Stunned, Holly watched in silent disbelief as the impact knocked Jake's head forward, then backwards. He fell on his backside, his head hitting the floor a millisecond later with a loud thud.

Dazed, Jake looked up at her.

"Holy Mother of God!" he gasped. "You've been shot!"

Confused, Holly dropped to her knees next to Jake with a piercing scream ringing in her ears. Blood pooled around his neck and left shoulder. His eyes closed.

"No! No! No!" Holly yanked at Jake's clean white shirt, popping buttons off as she pulled it open. She blanched at the oozing liquid, forgetting about Thomas Grapley. She had to put pressure on the wound.

Stop the bleeding.

She had to stop the bleeding.

Remembering how Jake had taken care of Dr. Sanchez, she ran to the washroom, grabbed a clean towel, folded it on her way back, then pressed it against Jake's chest.

Only then did she look up to find Thomas Grapley gone. The door swinging wide.

"Coward," she yelled after him, not knowing or caring if he heard.

Jake moaned as she applied more pressure. She

187

couldn't let him die. She couldn't lose him now. Not when they had just found each other.

"Don't you die on me, Daniels. Not now! Not ever!"

Holly recalled how Jake had turned the researcher's body over to examine it to see if the bullet had gone through. Awkwardly, she maintained pressure on the front of Jake's shoulder while turning him over as carefully as possible.

No blood!

Dear God! The bullet was lodged inside!

Tears streamed down her face unheeded. Her hands shook. She had to control the anxiety attack she felt coming on in spades.

She had to get help.

Holly rubbed at her tears with the back of her hand. She took a deep breath. Her head buzzed. There was no time to waste. Jake needed help. Now!

Holly ran to the phone and dialed the front desk. It took forever before someone answered, and then total confusion ensued. Finally, a sane English speaking voice came on the line.

"Please help. Mr. Daniels has been shot," Holly pleaded. "I need a doctor. An ambulance. Hurry!"

"We heard the shot. Police are on the way. Someone will be there soon."

Holly gave her room number, then hung up. She rushed back to Jake's side and reapplied pressure on the still-bleeding wound. She flinched as a sharp, piercing pain radiated down her right arm. She looked down. Lordy, her own arm, now throbbing painfully, was covered with blood.

"Oh, my God! I've been shot, too." Holly reeled back on the balls of her feet. She stared, transfixed at the blood trickling down her bare arm. How could she be shot? She hadn't felt a thing.

There hadn't been a second shot.

Stars flitted in front of her eyes. She swayed

Amazon Connection

backward, the swirling, psychedelic, twinkling lights growing stronger, brighter. She shut her eyes to stop the dizziness, then mustered all the courage she could find, and took a good look at her own wound. Relief washed over her shaking body. The bullet had merely grazed her arm.

Nothing compared to Jake's wound.

She put her head between bent knees and sucked in large quantities of air.

The world righted itself.

Suddenly paramedics were everywhere. Like a flutter of autumn leaves on a windy afternoon they rushed around her and Jake.

"Thank God you're here," she stated, reluctantly leaving Jake's side so they could set to work on him right away.

Two policemen swooped into the room.

"You are shot," the taller of the two said. "Sit."

Glad to have things under control and taken out of her hands, Holly did as she was told. The officer spoke to one of the medics in Portuguese, who quickly brought his bag over to the bed and immediately set to work on her wound. The antiseptic-smelling solution, and injection, stung like crazy.

Holly gritted her teeth. Tears sprang to her eyes.

"A couple stitches, maybe. We will take you to hospital soon. First we care for this one." He pointed to Jake who was lying unconscious on the floor, surrounded by the medics.

"Will he be okay?"

They ignored her as they continued to hover over him.

The officer again spoke to the medics then turned to her.

"The bleeding is stopped. He needs surgery to remove the bullet."

Carol Henry

Jake groaned when they lifted him onto the stretcher. Holly ran to his side, her legs like rubber bands that had been stretched one too many times. She cursed as the room began to tilt around her again. She grabbed for the first chair she came to and plunked down onto it. She could do nothing but watch as the men wheeled Jake from the room. She felt weak, tired. Holy crap! What was that injection they'd given her?

"I have to go with him," she insisted.

Her plea had little impact.

"You rest. You answer questions first, then we go to hospital."

"Ask on the way to the hospital."

"Sit a minute longer, Miss. It will be some time before the doctors are finished with your young man."

Holly obeyed. It seemed she didn't have a choice.

"Please. We do not want to waste time getting information about the man who shot you and your friend. We need to know what happened. The hotel and grounds are surrounded and are being searched as we speak, but it will help if you cooperate and give us additional information."

Holly filled the officer in on Harold and Thomas' scheme, Harold following them into the rainforest, shooting Dr. Sanchez, then kidnapping her. Thomas' part in all of it.

"We tried to talk Mr. Grapley into putting the gun down, and then everything happened all at once. I don't know what else I can tell you."

"This Thomas Grapley, he was staying at this hotel?"

Holly wanted to scream. She wanted Jake. She wanted to be by his side when he woke up.

"Miss Newman?"

Head buzzing, it took Holly a moment to realize the policeman had asked her a question.

190

"Yes." Holly rubbed her temples. The pain persisted.

"Do you know where he would go?"

"I have no idea. Perhaps to Colombia to look for Mr. Bennett."

"And this Mr. Bennett?"

"I suspect he's on his way to Tabatinga."

"Tabatinga? On the Colombian border, no? I will alert the authorities. Please describe these men for me?"

The description Holly gave was probably not an accurate one, given her biased point of view. But it was enough for someone to recognize the two men. The officer turned and spoke Portuguese to his partner, who rushed out the door.

Hopefully, to go after one or both of the gun-wielding, sleazy men.

Holly closed her eyes and laid her head back on the rim of the chair. She hoped they'd catch the rats. They deserved to be hung.

Over an alligator-infested bog.

Deep in the jungle.

Mere inches above the water.

"Come. I will take you to hospital now. Then you can see your friend."

Getting into the small cracker-box size police vehicle waiting for them, Holly accepted the officer's assistance. He opened the door, ushered her inside, then circled around the car, and got in behind the wheel.

"We will be there in a moment," he nodded at her through the rearview mirror.

The car jerked forward.

Holly's head flung forward, too.

The car went up on the curb, then down with a bump.

Holly's bottom lifted off the seat then back down hard. Her teeth rattled. Her headache spiked.

Carol Henry

The police officer applied pressure to the gas pedal. The car sped into the afternoon traffic.

Thoughts about fear, trust, commitment, risk, and blame all flew out the window. It was nothing compared to the pain of what her life would be like without Jake.

Chapter Twenty

Jake woke to a darkened room and a fuzzy head. It took several minutes for it to clear. The events leading up to his being in a hospital bed came crashing down around him. The sound of Holly's scream. The blood dripping down her arm. She'd been shot! He'd been helpless.

He shut his eyes and covered them with a shaky hand. Why the hell was he the one in a hospital bed with an I.V. sticking out of his left hand? He'd only heard one shot.

Where *was* Holly? He had to get up and find her.

Putting action to words, Jake threw the sheet back and swung his legs over the edge of the mattress. His head spun, his chest screamed with pain. The I.V. brought him up short. A bandage was wrapped tightly around his chest and left arm.

Damn it. What the hell happened?

Jake flopped back against the pillows with an agonized groan. His head swam and stars swirled behind closed lids.

Where the hell was Holly?

"Am I dreaming?" Jake asked when he opened his eyes later to find her standing next to his bed. "Have I conjured you up?"

"Relax, Jake. You're going to be okay."

Holly leaned over him and brushed her hand across his forehead.

Good Lord, he'd died and gone to heaven. Holly's beautiful face was mere inches from his. He leaned up and put his lips to hers. She nudged him back down into the pillow.

Then, sweet dreams of sweet dreams, she kissed him. He was literally floating on cloud nine and it had nothing to do with the medication they'd pumped into him. Holly was here. She was safe.

Jake drew his right arm up around Holly and pulled her into him. The hell with the bandages. He gently held her in place and devoured her lips. When breathing became necessary, he let her go.

But not far.

"Holly," he whispered. "My God! I saw blood dripping down your arm. What happened?"

"I'm fine, Jake. How are you feeling? You've been out a long time."

"My mouth is dry and my head is swimming."

Holly poured ice water into a small plastic cup, inserted a straw, and held it for him while he drank.

"Just a sip for now. You don't want to get sick and undo those stitches in your shoulder."

"I don't remember anything after I hit that floor." He shook his head, then looked into her eyes. "Except for the blood running down your arm. Are you hurt? What the hell happened?"

"I'm fine. A superficial wound. A couple stitches. That's all. I hardly feel the pain."

He didn't buy her laughter. Her face was drawn. Her skin pale and bruised. He didn't give a damn about himself. Or how superficial she thought her wound. She'd been through too much already. It was his fault she'd gotten hurt, kidnapped and shot at. She could have been killed. Again!

And she was worried about him?

He'd never forgive himself.

This whole project had done nothing but put Holly in danger.

Next time she might not be so lucky.

"Look, Holly, if those two men are still out there..."

Amazon Connection

"They're looking for Thomas now. As for Harold? With any luck, he never made it to Tabatinga."

"Don't bet on Bennett still being lost. Remember, he's got connections on the inside. I suspect either Temboni or Biozzo are in on their scheme. They stand to gain a lot of money."

"Why would you suspect them?"

"It makes sense. They had access to the government's maps, worked with Bennett and Grapley. If Bennett is alive..."

"Do you think he is?"

"Maybe. If he is, he'll want to get his hands on that money. What's he got to lose? He's already shot Dr. Sanchez and kidnapped you."

"We've got his gun. I turned it over to the police as evidence."

"Good girl. What happened after Grapley shot us? And what about Dr. Sanchez? How's he doing?"

Jake clutched her hand in his and drew it to his lips. Then tucked it under his chin. It was warm. Soft.

"Dr. Sanchez is stable and going to make it. They've moved him to a reconstruction home to keep an eye on him. As for both of us being hit, you're right, there was only one shot. When I realized Thomas was about to shoot you, I shoved you aside. The bullet nicked my arm. But you got hit anyway. Thomas panicked and ran out. Afterwards I stopped the flow of blood."

"You stopped the blood? You can't stand the sight of blood."

"I've seen enough of it to last a lifetime, that's for sure. But I couldn't let you lay there and bleed to death. I remembered how you helped Dr. Sanchez. I did the same. Then I called the front desk. They'd already heard the shot and had called the authorities. After that, it was a blur; the paramedics arrived and took you away. The police interviewed

195

me, then brought me to the hospital. It's been a hairy twenty-four hours. I've been so worried, Jake. But the doctor has assured me you're going to be fine. They got the bullet out. It missed the shoulder blade."

"You're a brave lady, Sweetheart. But you still need to be cautious until they catch those two."

If it wasn't for him, Holly would never have been stranded, lost and kidnapped. She deserved so much better than that.

So much better than him!

He wasn't kidding when he said trouble dogged him. As a troubleshooter for GlennCorp, it came with the territory.

What was he thinking getting involved with Holly? Putting her in such danger?

He looked into her emerald eyes sparkling with the many shades of the rainforest. And got a jolt when he saw the love staring back at him.

Love?

Yes. He loved her.

He loved her too much to put her in harms way again.

He had to let her go before their relationship became serious. He was already tied in knots. Just remembering how great it felt to make love to her, to hold her, to be wrapped in each others arms all night long. He craved her touch now.

But nothing could come of it.

He worked alone. And it was dangerous work.

He was about to break her heart, and it was tearing him apart.

He had to tell her the truth. She had to know.

"There's something I haven't told you about Bennett and Grapley's money laundering scheme."

Her smile and quiet trust made it hard for him to find the right words. Words that would soften the blow.

Amazon Connection

"You don't happen to own a Swiss bank account do you?"

"I don't think I like what you're suggesting, Jake. What's going on?" Holly pulled her hand from his and stepped back from his bedside.

He didn't blame her for giving him attitude.

He had to go on—get it over with. There was no other way.

"Besides the fact that they have an insider working with them, Derrick led me to believe that you might be involved."

"What!" Holly jumped back further from the bed. "You think I'm involved? You think I'm the insider?" she squeaked.

His insides knotted.

"I didn't say that, Holly."

She was making it too easy for him.

"But you do! You actually think I would do such a thing? No wonder you questioned my report. You didn't trust me?"

She was right, damn it. It was a matter of trust. He hadn't trusted her. On his behalf he hadn't known her well enough. She was just part of the job.

At first.

"Admit it, Holly. What proof did I have that you weren't involved?"

"What proof did you have that I was?"

He watched her walk away from him. She stood at the window, her back to him, her arms crossed in front of her, her head held high. Jake hesitated.

He knew he was about to twist the knife in her heart even deeper.

"You've spent time with all the parties involved," he counted out on his fingers. "You made GlennCorp's engineers change the route. They complied. And it turned out to be wrong. You gave a very convincing report to the delegation. It championed Bennett and Grapley's work. And there

197

was nothing, I repeat *nothing*, that so much as led us to believe that you weren't part of their scheme."

He couldn't leave it at that; he had to give her something.

"If it's any consolation, I've doubted your involvement from the beginning."

"You've been fishing for answers all along." She turned to face him. "You made it a point to get close to me. You made love to me hoping I would tell you everything you wanted to know."

He didn't deny it.

Tears streamed down her pale face. "You only made love to me hoping I would confess to being part of their plan. You used me, Jake! Admit it." She was standing over him now. Lord, he wanted to take her in his arms and take away the hurt he saw in her eyes.

He heard the disappointment in her low, accusing voice and almost gave in to his own chaotic emotions. Again, he had to give her something. He knew she was hurt enough to refuse to believe anything else he said.

"I didn't know you then. But from the moment I met you, I had a hard time believing you could be involved with the likes of them."

He was right. Her body language spoke volumes. He could see it in those tear-filled eyes.

"You used me, Jake. I'll never forgive you for that."

As much as he wanted to, he didn't deny it. How could he? It was for her own good.

"Derrick uncovered their plan. They were going to launder money from the project into a Swiss bank account. Your name was on that account. What was I to believe? Derrick sent me down to check out everything. Everyone. That meant you, too."

"My God, Jake! Is there anything else you're holding back? If it involves me I have a right to know."

Jake saw the heartache on her scratched and bruised face.

Damn it! He was such an ass!

"Not a thing, Holly. Not a thing."

Damn, he was tired. He couldn't stand to see the pain on her lovely face any longer. He closed his eyes. It didn't help. Her pain and hatred seeped into him. Letting her go, letting her believe he'd used her didn't feel as good as he'd expected.

He now knew what they meant when they said love hurt.

But he had to do whatever it took to keep her safe.

"Go home, Holly. You've seen what these men can do. This is no life for you. Get out of Brazil."

He heard the catch in her throat, the sob she tried to conceal, and her steps as she walked out of the room.

Out of his life.

It would have been easier if Grapley had just shot him straight through the heart.

Once Holly left Jake's room, she blindly rushed down the corridor and circled the empty wheelchair next to the nurses station. She ignored them when they called to see if she was okay. She didn't stop.

She turned the corner and just missed the stretcher with a lifeless body moaning in pain. She brushed at the flow of tears and ran down the hollow hallway. She threw the swinging doorway open and ran out into the hot humidity. After the air-conditioning inside, it was like a slap in the face. Much easier to deal with then the virtual one she'd just received from Jake Daniels.

How could he use her like that?

She could have sworn he had feelings for her. Real feelings. Could he have made love to her like that if he didn't feel something?

199

The fragrance of the tropics, the warmth of the bright afternoon sunshine, the loud traffic and boisterous pedestrians rushing to and fro were at odds with her emotional turmoil. Devastated by Jake's betrayal, throwing her love back in her face was the last straw. Nothing she'd been through equaled the pain she now suffered.

Holly let the tears trickle down her bruised cheeks. She found a wooden bench in a secluded part of the garden next to the hotel. She sat and wiped at her tears.

How had she let this happen to her? How had she let Jake Daniels get so entrenched in her heart in such a short period of time only to stomp on it like a pesky ant?

Hadn't she learned anything from her previous relationship with...what's his name?

Apparently not.

With a heavy heart, Holly dragged herself back inside the hotel and took the elevator up to the fourth floor. Her room was cordoned off with orange tape. A team of investigators were milling about. The spot where Jake had fallen after he'd been shot was marked on the floor. His blood now dry.

Holly shivered. The thought of Jake losing all that blood knotted her stomach. She had to keep telling herself Jake was all right now.

And he didn't love her.

In her present state of mind Holly had forgotten that the hotel had given her a new room. She'd automatically come to this one. The one she'd stayed in since coming to Brazil. It seemed ages ago, now.

Had her wild adventures in the rainforest with Jake really happened? Had she lain in Jake's arms all night long? Had they made love?

Was it only a dream?

Or was it wishful thinking on her part?

Obviously it hadn't meant a thing to him.

He hadn't denied her accusations.

Holly approached one of the officers next to the door.

They hadn't let her take anything out before, and she'd already bought an outfit in the hotel's boutique. Her funds were running low and she didn't want to have to splurge on yet another.

"Can I go inside to get my clothes?"

"*Pesaroso.* No," the officer apologized.

"But I need clean clothes."

"*Pesaroso,*" the man repeated. "I am sorry. We are not finished."

Holly heard the regret in the man's voice as he turned to speak to one of the other officers. She didn't know what was taking them so long to investigate the scene. Unless they thought she was involved with Harold and Thomas' scheme, too. Which was too wild to believe. After all, Harold had kidnapped her and Thomas had shot at her.

She wanted to go home, but she wasn't allowed to leave the country. The authorities had to work through the case.

Her sister was going to kill her if she didn't make it home in time for the wedding of the century. After all, she was the maid of honor. It was bad enough she'd missed the bridal shower.

Everything was falling apart around her. Things she didn't seem to have any control over.

She hated not being in control.

Holly trudged down to the third floor to her new room. Even while kidnapped and on her own in the rainforest, she hadn't felt this hopeless. How was she going to survive the fact that she had given herself, her heart—body and soul, to Jake Daniels?

Only to have him reject her?

Holly shut the door behind her. She quickly pulled the bolt and fastened the chain.

As rooms went, this one was even more upscale.

A fresh bowl of fruit decorated the small table behind the long wicker sofa in the middle of the suite. It filled the room with the fresh scent of citrus. A pitcher of ice water sat next to it. A bucket with crushed ice and a bottle of something she didn't even want to consider drinking until she'd had a decent meal was close by.

Along with two fluted crystal glasses.

She picked up a banana and peeled it on the way to the washroom. She looked in the mirror and froze. Staring back at her was a pale, drawn reflection of a tear-stained face. Dejection written all over it.

She groaned. The eyes looking back at her were as dull and as lifeless as a blind person's. According to the discolored smudges under her eyes she needed sleep. At least 24 hours worth.

She turned the shower taps on, peeled her clothes off, and stepped under the pulsating spray. She ripped the bandage off her arm and let the hot water cascade over her aching, tired body.

God, the hurt was unbearable, A steamroller couldn't cause this much pain. She hadn't been this hurt when she'd left...

...what was his name?

It didn't matter.

She had to forget all about Jake Daniels, now.

He was pond scum!

And she loved him.

Chapter Twenty-One

Jake woke more alert, but still in pain. He knew what he'd done to Holly was for her own good. He was no stranger to the dangers that surrounded him. It was part and parcel of his job.

It was his life.

True, he usually came out on top with barely a scratch, but that was the risk he took. Putting someone else's life in danger was another matter altogether. Especially when that someone was Holly. How had he let himself fall so completely in love with her? And in such a short period of time? He must have been crazy to have let it go that far.

He'd had no choice but to end it before it had gone any further.

Her safety was more important.

Jake pushed the breakfast tray aside. Just looking at the food made him sick to his stomach. He drank the tepid coffee in two long swallows, instead.

"I see they can't keep you down for long, Jake. How's it going?"

"Derrick! What are you doing here?"

People seemed to keep materializing out of nowhere every time he opened his eyes.

"I haven't been here very long. I got in late last night. I met with Mr. Delgado this morning. Everything is on track."

"Good. Now tell them I'm ready to get the hell out of here. I've had enough of this bed to last me a lifetime."

"From what I understand you lost a lot of blood.

I'm glad they operated and removed the bullet."

"It's no big deal. I'll live." ·

"Yes, but you still need to recuperate. This isn't Alaska, but you're getting a well-deserved rest."

"You should've let me go to Alaska in the first place. Sent Zimmer down instead. Now, help me up, will you? I want to use the facilities instead of that cold metal bed pan."

"A bit testy this morning, aren't we?"

"Just help me get up. My legs aren't shot up; I can still walk."

Still attached to the I.V. drip, Jake let Derrick pull the contraption along behind as he entered the small bathroom.

"Thanks," he muttered, when he got back in bed and pulled the sheet up around his waist. He lay back against the pillows and closed his eyes. The pain in his shoulder throbbed from the exertion.

"Are you all right?"

"Yeah. It only hurts when I breathe."

"What happened? What did you do to provoke Grapley, anyway?"

"Wish I knew. One minute I was taking a shower, the next thing I know he's holding a gun on me. I couldn't get close enough to jump him and take the gun away."

"I gathered Miss Newman had quite a time of it, as well. I'm glad to see she's come through unscathed. I'm also glad to learn she wasn't involved. A very nice lady, Holly Newman."

"Unscathed? You call being kidnapped and shot at unscathed? Bennett kidnapped her at gunpoint, pistol-whipped her, then dragged her into the jungle." Jake shut his eyes, remembering.

"She's safe now, Jake. She's safe." Derrick leaned forward in the chair next to the bed.

"No thanks to us. I should've trusted my instincts, Derrick. Trusted her. If I'd listened to her instead of suspecting her, none of this would have happened."

"You didn't have a choice. You had a job to do. You didn't know her. How the hell could you trust her?"

Jake opened his eyes when he heard Derrick chuckle. "What's so funny?" He didn't see the humor in any of it. Especially Holly's involvement.

"Sorry. I was just thinking of the conversation I had with Ms. Newman earlier. She gave me a piece of her mind. Seems she blames me for a lot of things, namely, sending you out into the wilds of the Amazonian jungle and putting *your* life in danger. There was more, but that's the crux of it. She made it clear she doesn't blame you for what happened to her out there. Although she didn't give details, she insisted it was her own fault."

"She would. If I'd only been more insistent that she not go. If I'd only known..."

"Sounds like you have a fireball on your hands, Daniels."

"Not after last night. My job is too dangerous. You know it and I know it. I can't knowingly put her in any more danger. I refuse to."

"Yep, you've got it bad."

"It's not over yet. Those two slime-balls are still out there. She was kidnapped once. I want a 24/7 watch on her until those men are caught!"

Jake didn't wait for Derrick to respond. He had to make sure Holly was safe.

"You've got to promise me you'll get protection for her, Derrick," he demanded. "Get her out of Brazil. Send her back to New York."

"And you think she'll listen to me? Relax. I've already made arrangements for her protection. Yours, too. Right now I'm on my way to pay Temboni and Biozzo a visit. See if they'll talk. If they think Bennett and Grapley have double-crossed them and left them to hang, they might give us something to work with."

"Those two must have discovered I was going out to check the route and visit Sanchez, and told Bennett and Grapley. The first inkling I had that something was wrong was when we were stranded. Then, when I tried to follow the map and got lost, my hunch got stronger. I was thoroughly convinced of it when we ended up next to the *Vale de Javari.*"

Derrick whistled. "Not a great start, but certainly revealing. Then what happened?"

Jake continued to fill Derrick in on all that had taken place, up to and including the incident with Grapley in Holly's room.

"Discovering Holly kidnapped at gunpoint was the worst day of my life," he told Derrick. "There was blood everywhere. I didn't know if it was Holly's or Bennett's. I knew he had a gun and he'd already shot Sanchez, who by the way I understand is going to live. He'll be able to testify against Bennett."

Jake leaned back in bed, his head starting to buzz again. She might be safe now, but because of him, Holly'd been shot. Okay, so it wasn't a deep or serious wound—this time. The fact of the matter was she'd been shot. He didn't like that one bit.

"If you've already talked to Holly, then she's told you what happened after Grapley shot us."

"Yes, she filled me in on that. When I didn't hear back from you Friday morning, I changed all the codes, effectively shutting him out of all our accounts. It must have pushed him over the edge. I guess I'm just as much to blame for getting your lady shot."

Jake ignored Derrick's implications that Holly was his lady. It wasn't going to happen now.

"I have another meeting with Mr. Delgado in about an hour. We're going to go talk to Biozzo and Temboni. You try and get some rest. I'll take it from here and check back with you later."

"Just see about getting me out of here. And get me a ticket to Alaska, for God's sake."

His plea fell on deaf ears as Derrick walked out the door. Jake pounded the bed with his right fist, then reached over and pressed the red call button.

He needed something to kill the pain.

Chapter Twenty-Two

Holly hadn't been looking for love. She certainly didn't believe in love at first sight. But Jake Daniels had blind-sided her. And look where it had gotten her.

She sat up in bed. It was no use trying to get any rest, her mind kept reeling with the fact that Jake had used her. How had she missed the signs?

Right. They'd been there. She just hadn't been looking for any.

Actually, he'd had to spell it out for her. She'd been such a fool.

Again!

Holly rolled over in bed. She should never have followed Jake into that jungle.

But she had.

And she had to put it behind her and move on.

It hurt like hell.

She forced back tears, refusing to let them fall. Instead, she got up and made a pot of coffee. The aroma of the rich brew and the effects of the caffeine helped clear her mind.

She stood by the window and looked out over the center courtyard. Only one question remained. Why?

Why didn't Jake admit to using her? To making love to her in order to get information from her?

Why?

Why had he suddenly become cold, almost uncaring. And then tell her he hadn't believed she was part of Bennett and Grapley's scheme?

It didn't make sense.

Amazon Connection

Holly sat up with a jolt!

The rat! He thought he was responsible for her nearly being killed. He was trying to protect her.

By pushing her aside.

By lying to her!

Well, if Jake Daniels thought he was going to get away with that, he was sadly mistaken. Drugged and under the influence of the turn of events the last few days he may be, but clearly he didn't understand how strong her tenacity was when faced with a challenge. If he hadn't learned that about her on their walk on the wild side, then he hadn't learned anything about her at all.

But he was going to learn.

Sending her running away like a frightened puppy with its tail tucked between its legs was about to come back and bite him in the butt. He'd caught her off guard. Too much had happened between them. She hadn't been thinking. She'd been so excited to see him awake and eager to be held in his arms. She hadn't expected the curveball that had set her head spinning and her heart breaking.

But her mind was clear now. Jake *did* have feelings for her.

She'd followed him into the jungle. She'd been surrounded by a tribe of wild Indians. She'd been kidnapped at gunpoint, and after escaping Harold Bennett's clutches, had spent the night in the jungle.

Alone!

If that hadn't frightened her away from him, what made him think anything he could say now would? She loved him, damn it. And she suspected he loved her, too.

Or at least had strong feelings for her. Why else would he go out of his way to try to shield her from more danger? Why else would he push her away, and tell her to go home?

He hadn't confessed to using her.

209

Carol Henry

Okay, so it had taken her long enough to figure it out. It was because he *hadn't* used her.

Being held in his arms, making love to him, had been worth all the risks she'd taken out there in the jungle. Wasn't it worth one more risk now? He was good at setting down challenges. Now let's see how well he accepted them. She was going to march straight back to that hospital room and confront him. Make him tell her, make him admit, if he dared, that the words she'd put in his mouth weren't true.

The phone rang, startling her out of her contemplations. She picked up the receiver. "Hello."

"Hello, Ms. Newman. It's Derrick Holmes. I've just come from the hospital..."

"Is it Jake? Oh, my God, is he okay? Has something happened?" Heart racing, Holly closed her eyes expecting bad news. Jake had been fine when she'd left him earlier. What if he'd had a turn for the worst?

What if their argument had caused something to go wrong?

"Jake is okay. Trust me, they can't wait to get rid of him."

Holly released her breath slowly, and sat down to keep from falling over.

"I called to tell you the contracts are signed. Mr. Temboni and Mr. Biozzo were both arrested earlier today for their part in assisting Bennett and Grapley. Mr. Delgado has been keeping his eye on them for sometime, as well. The authorities were able to apprehend them without incident."

"Are you sure it's them? They were such gentlemen."

"Quite. They confessed when they learned of Bennett and Grapley's escapades with attempted murder and kidnapping. They wanted no part of that. They were only in it for the money. They were

210

too willing to confess."

"What about Harold Bennett and Thomas Grapley?"

"The authorities found an unidentified body not far from Tabatinga. They suspect it's Bennett's."

"Does Jake know?"

"Not yet. I'm on my way there to tell him now."

"What about Grapley?"

"They'll find him. I'm sorry you've gotten involved, Miss Newman. We didn't mean for it to go this far. I'll have someone let you know as soon as Grapley has been apprehended."

"Thank you."

Holly hung up relieved to know that Bennett had been found. It would only be a matter of time before they had Thomas Grapley. There was nothing to keep her in Brazil any longer.

Except Jake.

She had to talk to Jake before she left Brazil.

But first she had to make plane reservations to fly back home now that she could leave the country. As luck would have it, she was able to get a flight out on Wednesday afternoon, with connections that would get her back to New York very early Friday morning. She'd be cutting it short, but she'd make the wedding on Saturday.

Next she called her sister. Thankfully the answering machine clicked on saving Holly from having to listen to her sister's hysterics when she found out Holly would be cutting it close. Saving her call to Wild and Wonderful for last, she dialed Marcia's number. Marcia was cool, calm, and collected, which helped to calm Holly's own chaotic frame of mind.

"I'm glad to hear everything is finished down there. I'm sorry I didn't get back to you about Mr. Daniels, but I wasn't able to get in touch with Mr. Holmes at GlennCorp. Apparently his wife had a baby and he wasn't taking calls."

"He actually came down here and signed the contracts this morning. Tell Helen I'll be home by the end of the week."

"She's still in China somewhere. I haven't been able to get in touch with her either. I'm starting to get worried."

"I wouldn't worry about Helen. She can take care of herself."

"I hope you're right. I'll see you on Monday, then?"

"Monday."

With everything organized and taken care of, Holly hung up the phone in much better spirits.

Now to tackle Jake Daniels.

About to slip into her shoes, she heard a loud thud at the door followed by grunts and groans. Holly ran to look through the security hole.

Holy moly!

Thomas Grapley! He'd come back!

To finish the job?

Thomas Grapley was outside scuffling with one of the security guards. He appeared limber and quick for his size, and she was surprised to see that he had the upper hand.

Holly quickly stepped back from the door.

Had he seen her?

No. It wasn't possible.

She flew back to the door and leaned closer to the miniature porthole. She slowly scanned the hallway. The other guard was lying on the floor. He got back up and shook his head. The incident appeared unbelievably surreal as Thomas Grapley attacked first one and then the other man.

Holly ran to the phone and called the front desk.

"Help! I need help! Three men are fighting outside my room."

"They are security guards, ma'am. They have

already called for backup."

Thank God!

Holly hung up and ran back to the door. This time Thomas Grapley's contorted face was pressed up against the glass hole, his eye level with hers. It was bloodshot, huge, and pissed off.

She shrieked and jumped back, sure he had seen her this time.

She heard his body slide down the door. Mustering up the nerve to look out again, she saw him bend over and jam his head into the other man's midsection. The two of them hurtled across the floor and banged into the concrete wall.

The guard lying on the floor finally managed to stand. But when he sprinted toward Grapley, Grapley merely kicked the guard between the legs, effectively putting him back down on the floor. Like lightening, Grapley turned back to the other security guard and had him twisted and shoved up against her door.

Who was this madman?

And where were the police? What was taking them so long?

That did it! Holly grabbed the fist thing she could find—a large, heavy ceramic lamp. She pulled the plug out of its socket and headed back to the door. She turned the lock and yanked the door open.

And stepped aside as the security guard fell on his back in the doorway. Not missing a beat, Holly brought the lamp down hard on Thomas Grapley's head. Large chunks of pink glass went flying.

"You bitch!" he moaned, reaching for her.

Grapley teetered, leering at her, then fell with a muffled thump on top of the stunned guard. The second guard rushed forward, breathless. He pulled out his handcuffs and shackled Grapley's hands behind his back. The click of the cuffs being locked in place was music to Holly's ears.

The guard pulled Grapley off his partner's prone, groaning body.

"He is fast, this one," the guard managed, trying to catch his breath. "Be careful not to cut your feet on the broken lamp."

Holly looked down. In all the commotion she hadn't had time to put her shoes on.

Heavy, rushing footsteps filled the corridor. Holly turned to see several uniformed men descending on them, weapons drawn. They were a little late, but it was a relief to see them.

And to know it was all over.

Adrenalin pumped throughout her system. Her whole body shook. Holly stepped over a large chunk of ceramic, leaned against the wall, and shut her eyes. Thomas Grapley moaned as they dragged his limp body down the hallway toward the elevator.

Relieved, she watched him disappear around the corner.

She came away from the wall, feet apart. And stopped breathing. Her heart skipped a beat.

Was she dreaming?

What the hell was Jake Daniels doing out of the hospital?

Chapter Twenty-Three

Rooted to the floor, Holly's insides churned with the need to run to him. She watched in anticipation as he slowly walked toward her. He walked close to the wall, barely touching it. Derrick Holmes walked on his other side for support.

Jake's poker face persona was missing. His eyes never left her face. He tried to smile, but his tight jaw and pale face kept it from happening. He stumbled and reached for the wall with his good hand. Derrick reached for him, but Jake shook his help away. He said something to Derrick. Derrick smiled and stepped away. Jake took a deep breath and came toward her. His face white behind his golden tan.

Even now he looked sinfully handsome.

His shirt almost hid his bandages. The empty sleeve gave his injuries away. Her heart ached for him. He should be back at the hospital resting. He'd just had surgery to remove a bullet for heaven's sake.

She looked over at Derrick Holmes. He said something to Jake she couldn't hear, then looked over at her, shrugged his shoulders, then smiled. Holly looked back at Jake.

Jake wasn't smiling.

Holly wrung her hands the closer he came. The stern look on his face was softened by the dark locks hanging over his forehead. Her heart melted and she took a step forward. He stopped and looked into her eyes. She held her breath waiting for him to speak.

He drew her into his arms and kissed her.

A pulse-stopping kiss.

Holly's head reeled. She returned the kiss, telling him in no uncertain terms that she reciprocated his feelings.

"They got Grapley," Holly managed, her voice shaky "They just took him away."

"I know. I saw him."

He kissed her again, pulled her close and leaned on her for support. She braced herself against the wall and kissed him back.

"We need to talk, Holly," Jake whispered, pulling her closer. "When Derrick told me Grapley was spotted in the hotel I made him get me the hell out of the hospital. I warned you, I told you he'd be back. I had to come and make sure you were okay."

"It's over now. I'll be fine."

Jake held her, both of them careful of each other's injuries.

Someone cleared their throat behind them.

Holly and Jake turned to see Derrick leaning against the outside railing against a tropical backdrop.

"I guess the two of you don't need me hanging around," Derrick said. "I have a plane to catch and a new baby to get back to, anyway." He came forward and shook Jake's good hand. "Take your time, Daniels. Don't rush back. Now that the project is on track, I'll be spending a bit of time with the new baby. Consider yourself on vacation. I'll catch up with you later."

"Much later," Jake said, turning back to Holly, ignoring Derrick's departure.

Holly didn't figure Derrick needed a response from her either. And didn't mind at all when Jake drew her in for another explosive, hungry kiss.

If Jake Daniels thought he was going to distract her with those mind-blowing kisses, he had another think coming. Mr. Sinfully Handsome wasn't going to get off the hook that easily. As much as she relished being held in his arms and being kissed like there was no tomorrow, she was still angry with him.

"I'm thinking I need bed rest," Jake wiggled his eyebrows at her.

"You have some explaining to do." Holly tugged at his good hand and pulled him through the open door. "Watch the glass."

Jake looked down at the broken ceramic pieces littering the carpet. "You really pack a punch, Sweetheart."

"Keep that in mind, Daniels. You're not out of the woods yet."

She watched his face turn serious.

"I've caused you nothing but trouble, Holly? If it wasn't for me you wouldn't have been shot."

"It wasn't your fault."

"You're letting me off the hook too easily. Trouble is what I do for a living. I wasn't kidding when I said danger follows me. I'm dangerous to be around. Hanging around me will only get you hurt."

"After what we shared back at the village, you're telling me you don't want to be around me?"

"That's not what I meant. You're mixing up my words."

"Are you telling me I was nothing but a one-night-stand? That you don't have feelings for me, Jake Daniels?"

"No! I mean yes, I have feelings for you. And no, I don't want to see you get killed because of me."

"Tell me the truth, Jake. Were you using me? Did you make love to me in order to get me to talk?"

"The truth is, Sweetheart, I did try to get close to you to find out what you knew, and to figure out if you were involved. But I started doubting myself after the first night we met. When I sat across the table from you and looked into your amazing emerald eyes. When we got stuck in the water-hibiscus patch on Lake January and you wrapped your arm through mine for protection, I was lost. I felt like such an ass for scaring you half to death, but I'd hoped you'd change your mind about coming with me. On the one hand I didn't want you there, but on the other, I wanted to see more of you. I've kicked myself several times for giving in to you. I knew how hard it would be for you, but I didn't know just how vulnerable you were. Despite being scared to death of everything that had to do with the jungle you still followed me out there and showed such courage and tenacity, that I found myself falling in love with you."

He pulled her close as tears streamed down her face.

"Ah, Sweetheart. No matter what obstacles we faced out in that jungle, you always rallied after the initial setback. And when Bennett kidnapped you and dragged you off, it was as if someone had stabbed me in the heart. I was helpless. And when I couldn't find you, I thought you were dead. Finding you back at the village, laying on our bedroll was like finally reaching that pot of gold at the end of the rainbow."

He gently held her from him. Using his thumb from his good hand, he wiped at her tears.

"Here, I have something for you." He reached in his bandaged arm and pulled out her feathered earring.

"Oh, Jake! You found it. I thought I lost it in the rainforest."

"It was in the cabin. God, when I walked in and found you gone, I knew it was my fault. Please forgive me, Holly. I'm sorry. I didn't mean to hurt you."

Hearing Jake say he was sorry recalled the

dream she'd had the first night in the jungle. She'd been wrapped in his arms then, too. She'd felt safe, and secure when she'd woken up then.

And she did now.

She pulled away and wiped at her own tears. "Did you just tell me you loved me?"

"Yes. I know it seems so soon, and I did try to fight it. But believe me, I wasn't using you, Holly. Especially when we made love."

"I love you, Jake. You've shown me a side of me that I didn't know existed. I'm stronger than I thought. I can deal with the unknown, thanks to you. I realize I can take care of myself and that I don't have to be afraid of things that go bump in the night."

"Blame it on everything that happened to us out in the jungle if you want, but as far as I'm concerned, Sweetheart, you're a born survivor. And one hell of a woman. Ever been to Alaska?"

"No, but I hear the scenery is lovely."

"So's the fishing. Care to join me?"

"I have a wedding to attend. Care to meet my family?"

"That could be arranged."

Jake left her side to lock the door and shut the drapes. He returned to her side and frog-marched her toward the bed. He held her in a tight embrace, then kissed her. Holly felt his body tremble and knew it wasn't just from the kiss. He really did need bed rest.

"Jake, I think we should take things slow. Really get to know each other. Find out more about each other..."

"Shhh. Listen. I think I hear the call of the bed."

"You mean *The Call of the Wild.*"

"Hmmm. How wild are we talking?" he whispered, wiggling his eyebrows.

"I meant you're confusing titles."

Carol Henry

"I'm not confusing anything, Sweetheart. Come here and I'll show you."

They'd reached the bed and Jake had her half naked and laying down beside him before she knew it.

"Doesn't your shoulder hurt?" she asked between kisses.

"The only thing I'm feeling right now, Sweetheart is you."

Thank you for purchasing this Wild Rose Press
publication. For other wonderful stories of romance,
please visit our on-line bookstore at
www.thewildrosepress.com.

For questions or more information contact us at
info@thewildrosepress.com.

The Wild Rose Press
www.TheWildRosePress.com